PAIGE HARTWICK

Discovery
Book One of the Cork Chronicles

First edition

ISBN: 979-8-9893694-0-9

This book was professionally typeset on Reedsy.
Find out more at reedsy.com

This is to for everyone out there who has ever been told that they're not good enough or had someone crush their hopes and dreams. You've got this!

I want to give a special thanks to 8 special men- Thank you for being my reason to STAY! Also, thank you Stay for encouraging me to follow my dreams. Now, hopefully, this series will help inspire you to follow your own dreams- or at least give you a short escape from reality.

Contents

CHAPTER ONE

"Hey, Kyra! You need to clean the bathrooms before you can leave tonight!" Meghan yelled as Kyra was already walking out the door.

"*Why*?! That was Sarah's job! Plus, I already clocked out…" Kyra was having an extremely bad day. Anything that could go wrong, had, and she was ready to just crawl in bed and cry herself to sleep.

"I honestly don't care! If you don't do it then you're fired! End of story!" Meghan yelled as she rolled her eyes. You know, for a supervisor, she was a total *bitch*! Kyra was always bending over backwards for everyone, just because she really needed the job.

"Then I'm clocking back in because, by law, you can't make me work for free. Don't worry though, I'll be done in less than thirty minutes. You can even time me if you're really *that* worried," she exclaimed as she walked back inside. The customers that were sitting at their tables, enjoying their food, had stopped to stare and watch the whole encounter. Kyra could feel the heat in her cheeks and could only imagine how red her face was. She was close to tears by that point, but she knew it would get so much worse if she showed any sign of weakness. Kyra was sick and tired of being treated like a slave, barely making minimum wage ($11 per hour).

As she was scrubbing the toilets, she came to the conclusion that as soon as she got home, she wasn't going to cry and give up. Instead, she would be applying for more jobs. Why should she settle for a shitty job when she knew she had unused talents that were going to waste? She used that frustration to clean the bathrooms faster than she ever had. It only took her twelve minutes… Kyra walked past Meghan and gave her the most blank look possible while she was clocking out.

The second the door closed behind her after walking outside, Kyra took a deep breath and looked out at the mountains and the town below. The trees had just begun to burst into fall colors. Just the sight of them and the smell of the crisp fall air always cheered her up. Kyra was hopeful she could find a job where she could work outside in nature somewhere, even if it was as an intern or something like that.

Ever since she was little, she always felt a closeness to nature- almost like it whispered her name as the wind blew by.

As she was about to get in her car, a woman that she had seen in the restaurant walked outside.

"Excuse me, miss?" She asked so sweetly, in a way that reminded her of her own grandmother who was back in Ireland.

"Yes, ma'am? Is everything alright?" She asked in response with her slight accent- her voice cracking right at the end.

"Actually, I was about to ask you the same thing," she said as she chuckled nervously. "I overheard the conversation between you and that witch- pardon my language. I saw the look on your face and it 'bout damn near broke my heart!" The older woman's eyes began to well up with tears.

"It's okay, I'm used to it," Kyra shrugged and sighed. "This is about an everyday thing. I've just learned to grin and bear it, but still stand up for myself a little bit."

"Still! She has NO right to treat you- or any other employee- like that! It just grinds my gears when some people think they can be nasty towards others. With that attitude of hers, I wouldn't be surprised if she were a slave owner in another life." Kyra chuckled at that.

"Do you plan on sticking it out here, or do you have another job lined up? My granddaughter might know of some places that are currently hiring. She's still inside with her grandfather- I could have her write them down for you before you leave, if you'd like," she told her. She was so compassionate.

"That would be very nice of her, thank you. I'm actually going to be applying for more jobs when I get home, whether I'm qualified or not. After the day I've had, I've decided that this will be my last week. I still live at home and I've already discussed it with my parents. They're willing to help me out until I find something else." Kyra felt like once she had started to speak, the words kept pouring out and she couldn't stop. It was just so nice that a complete stranger was interested in her well-being, especially when her own mother was only worried about the loss of her income.

"Well good for you! That sounds like a solid plan. It's a good thing your family is so caring and willing to help you instead of letting you struggle," the older woman said with her hand on her heart and had started to cry. "Can I give you a hug?" Kyra nodded and the woman gave her a huge hug, just as Meghan walked outside.

"What the *hell* is going on out here?! Kyra! Why are you still here? You need to leave! *NOW*! If you don't, I'll call the cops and they'll charge you with trespassing! I know because my dad is a cop. Now shoo, you filthy rat!" *Oh boy*! This bitch *definitely* had a death wish! What the hell was her problem?!

"Now listen here, bitch! She has done absolutely *nothing* to you! What the hell do you have against her, besides the fact that she's prettier than you?!" The older woman interjected. Kyra stood there, stunned. What was she supposed to do? Call the cops? No one had ever shown her so much animosity before.

Something caught Kyra's eye and she squinted to see what it was. It was what she assumed to be the woman's granddaughter filming the confrontation. She looked even closer and could see a man watching them while he was on the phone. She assumed he was calling the police- hopefully.

"She's a soulless slut that needs to go back to whatever shitty country she came from! Nobody wants her here! By the way, bitch, I'm *way* prettier than her! Redheads are the *ugliest* people and they should be exterminated! They're the devil's spawn!" Meghan screamed at the top of her lungs. Kyra thought Meghan would start foaming at the mouth at any moment from the way she was acting. It was kind of comical.

The joke was on her though because of the other people in the restaurant. Kyra could hear sirens in the distance. She'd had just about *enough* of Meghan's racist, bitchy attitude. Kyra and the older woman were both hoping that she'd be arrested as soon as the cops got there. Make her explain to her father why she's been physically and verbally abusing one of her employees for months on end to the point where that employee had attempted suicide more than once.

The woman that had come to Kyra's defense was in utter shock. She had never in her life heard someone say something so racist- and she was even from the deep south! She knew she needed to stick around until the cops got there and arrested Meghan. She looked over at Kyra to see that she appeared like she was mere seconds away from fainting.

"What, no witty comeback? Miss, 'I know everything.' See, I'm even smarter than you'll ever be! Dumb bitch! Granny here won't be able to protect you once you leave!" Meghan sneered at them both. Kyra couldn't help but let out a nervous laugh.

"Is that so? If you were truly smarter than me, then you would've realized that you're being filmed *and* the cops are almost here. Just so you know, Meghan, I *will* be pressing harassment charges and you *will* go to jail. I may not have been born here, but at least I was smart enough to study the laws in school. Also, if you were smarter than me, then you would know that I've been documenting everything for months. Have fun rotting in jail…"

By this point, Kyra was an anxious mess. She had her arms crossed in front of her so she could hide how badly she was shaking. Right as Meghan went to open her disgusting mouth again, the cops pulled into the parking lot. Kyra and the older woman looked at each other and let out a huge sigh of relief in unison. Kyra hadn't realized she had been holding her breath through most of the altercation.

Two of the cops walked over to Kyra. To her it felt like she was in a tunnel and couldn't understand a single word they were saying, and everything was in slow motion. Everything became blurry and she could feel herself falling. Her head hit the pavement and her vision faded to black.

Two

CHAPTER TWO

Kyra woke up to a siren that seemed to be piercing her skull. She looked around her, but nothing looked familiar. As she came out of the groggy haze, she realized that someone was talking to her. Then it hit her, she was in an ambulance…

"Good, you're awake! Can you tell me your name?" The paramedic asked.

"Kyra Walsh… What happened?! Why am I in an ambulance?" She asked as she was starting to panic. She was trying to calm herself because the faster her heart raced, the worse the pounding got in her head.

"Try and stay calm. We were told that you had collapsed and hit your head after an altercation at your job. Does any of that sound familiar to you?" It felt like his eyes were looking into her soul. It was probably from the head injury and slight amnesia, but the paramedic seemed strangely familiar. He looked like he might be close to her age, but it was hard to tell.

He had light brown hair that was just long enough to fall in his eyes. Those eyes were the brightest green she had ever seen. He seemed like he was tall and very athletic. She shook off the feeling and pushed the thought to the back of her mind.

She shook her head because the last thing she could remember was cleaning the bathrooms at work. After that it was nothing but blank. She could feel the memory like it was tickling the back of her brain, but it was just barely out of reach.

"Well, since you know your name, maybe you can answer a few medical questions for me? Any history of blackouts or seizures? What about anxiety or depression?" The tone of his voice made her stomach do a flip. It felt like they were two old friends that had known each other their whole lives…

"As far as I know, no seizures, but I was diagnosed with severe anxiety when I was twelve. I've never blacked out from it though, just major dizzy spells." Kyra felt like she really needed to remember what had happened…

The ambulance suddenly stopped and the doors were being opened. They were at the entrance to the emergency room. The paramedics wheeled her in to the ER, and for the next several hours, Kyra was poked and prodded by a revolving door of nurses and doctors. Then it was time for her MRI…

Kyra had never had an MRI before, but she had seen enough doctor shows to know that people with claustrophobia hated it. She made sure to let her doctor know so he could have one of the nurses give her something to help her relax. The nurses wheeled her to imaging and helped her into the machine. Kyra's palms were sweaty and her heart began to race. There was *no* way she was going to go through this ordeal again, so she closed her eyes and took a few slow, deep breaths.

"Okay, Kyra, try to stay as still as possible. It'll be over before you know it. Just try to go to your happy place," the technician said through the speaker.

"O-okay…" Kyra replied in a shaky voice. The machine started up and she was startled by the whirring, clunking sound. Kyra focused on the pattern of the sounds and took slow, even breaths to keep herself calm.

After a few minutes she started to feel drowsy, but she needed to stay awake. As a coping method, she started watching *Mulan* in her head. *Mulan* had been Kyra's favorite movie growing up because she wanted to be brave and heroic just like her.

About halfway through the movie, the machine started to power down and Kyra immediately relaxed.

"Are we done? Please tell me we don't have to do it again…" Kyra asked.

"We're all done! Your nurse will take you back to your room now. The neurologist will come talk to you as soon as he can go over your scans. It shouldn't take too long, maybe an hour at the most," the technician informed her. She was so worn out that she was looking forward to getting back to her room and taking a nap. But, as her luck would have it, her family and a cop were waiting for her out in the hall.

"*Kyra Rose Walsh*! What on earth happened? Your boss called us saying that you collapsed and had to be rushed to the hospital!" Kyra's mom, with her fiery red hair flowing down to her waist, asked impatiently. She looked like a wildfire- like she was ready to burn the world down to find out who hurt her daughter. It was a look that Kyra hadn't seen on her before. It felt foreign to her and out of place.

"Excuse me, ma'am? I need to speak with Ms. Walsh and get her statement while the incident is still fresh in her mind."

"Um, officer?… I can't remember anything. The last thing I remember was cleaning the bathrooms at work, then waking up in the ambulance. The doctor said that it might be stress induced amnesia, but he wouldn't know for sure until my scans came back." She started to slur her words and it was becoming really hard to keep her eyes open.

"Ms. Walsh really needs to rest now, Officer. Would she be able to wait until morning to give her statement? She might be able to remember more once she's gotten some sleep," Kyra's nurse told the officer. By this point, Kyra was so exhausted that her whole body was hurting and she felt like throwing up. Before she could even try to say anything, everything went black once again.

CHAPTER THREE

Kyra could hear people talking, but it was as if they were whispering at the end of a really long tunnel. She tried to open her eyes, but it felt as if her whole body had been encased in lead- like she were underwater, trying to claw her way to the surface. The voices began to fade and the darkness washed over her once again.

CHAPTER FOUR

"Kyra… Sweetie? It's time to wake up now… Please wake up. Máthair loves you so much!" Mrs. Walsh was crying while holding Kyra's hand between hers. She was trying to be strong for her baby girl, but seeing her laying there unconscious in the hospital bed, hooked up to all the monitors, was just too much to handle and she broke down.

Her son and youngest daughter were fast asleep in a couple of chairs in the corner. They had been crying all night and had only just fallen asleep. Her husband was back in Ireland on a business trip, so she'd wait and call him once his meeting was over. She knew that this meeting was very important for Mr. Walsh and that he'd need to be completely focused.

"Máthair? Cá bhfuil mé? Cén fáth a bhfuil tú ag gol?[1] Momma? Please don't cry." Kyra pleaded in a raspy voice. She looked around the room at the bland colored walls and generic printed pictures. The strong smell of disinfectant hit her like a brick wall. She looked down and could see the needle in the back of her hand. There were wires attached to her head and chest that were sticking out from under the hospital gown. She began to go into a full-blown panic at this point. What the hell was going on?! Why was she in the hospital?

"Sweetie, calm down. Take a deep breath and try to relax while I go get the doctor. Just lay still and I'll be right back." Kyra's mom kissed her forehead and left the room, her red hair blowing backwards with the sudden rush of her running from the room.

Her brother and sister were still asleep in the corner when all of a sudden the hair on the back of her neck stood on end and she felt like she was being watched. She couldn't see anyone out in the hallway so she shook it off and tried to relax. She went back to focusing on her breathing while she waited for her mom to come back in with the doctor.

"Sister! You're awake!" Kyra's sister Chloe yelled, running over to her bedside and giving her a big hug. Kyra buried her face in her sister's thin, blonde hair and took a deep breath. Her little sister's presence always helped to quell her panic attacks. She was her favorite person in the whole world. She was so small for her age and innocent; easily impressionable.

"I could say the same for you, silly goose," Kyra chuckled as she continued holding her sister. Chloe was only eleven years old, so she could only imagine how she was feeling, seeing her big sister laying there attached to so many machines. Kyra had Chloe sit in the bed with her and kept hugging her until their mother walked back in with the doctor a few minutes later.

"Well, hello there, Kyra. How're you feeling? I'll have to say, you were asleep for a bit longer than expected," the doctor said to Kyra.

"I feel fine. Now, can you *please* tell me what happened? The last thing I remember is walking in to work today. Wait, what day is it?! How long have I been asleep?!" Kyra started to have yet another panic attack and it felt as if her heart were about to beat out of her chest or stop altogether. Her fingers turned to ice and it became difficult for her to breathe as it felt as if someone had sat on her chest. The doctor called for the nurse and had her give Kyra something to calm her down. Once her heart rate slowed down, her doctor sat down and began answering her questions.

"Now, to answer your last question, you were unconscious for nearly thirteen hours. I was hoping that- with some sleep- your memory would come back, but it seems that your mind has blocked out even more of yesterday as some part of self-preservation. Which is unfortunate, but that doesn't necessarily mean it'll be permanent.

"There are some things we can try to get your memory back, but it's possible that it will come back all on its own. I would like to keep you here overnight for observation. Your only physical injuries are the scrapes on your hands and your head where you hit it on the pavement but those should heal up nicely over the next week or so. Your head is going to be sore for a couple of weeks, and you may have a few migraines, but other than that, you're in pretty good health."[2]

Kyra was so overwhelmed that she couldn't think of anything to ask the doctor. She had memory issues whenever it came to her anxiety and she hated having to record any doctor visits so she could recall information at a later time. It was like her brain would leave her body and go on vacation.

What if my memories never come back? Would Meghan just get to walk away, even with video proof and witnesses?

One thing was glaringly obvious. She'd need to find a new job- and sooner rather than later. Even though her parents had already agreed to help her out, that was before Meghan turned their worlds upside down.

Unbeknownst to the Walsh family, the events of the day before would be the last time that Kyra would play by their rules. She was sick and tired of everyone in her life always taking advantage of her kindness. Even more so- she was sick and tired of her parents treating her like a child. She was almost twenty-two for crying out loud! She loved her parents so much, but she was tired of them holding her back from becoming a better person. She was tired of all the gas lighting and manipulation. She was tired of being told to just 'think happy thoughts' and to quit being lazy all the time.

There was something big coming, she could feel it in her gut. She was scared, but more excited than anything. She just hoped that whatever was coming, that it would be something good and positive. There had been so much negativity in her life over the past several years that she felt like she was long overdue for some happiness.

CHAPTER FIVE

A few weeks later, Kyra had gone back home, was seeing a therapist twice a week to help with her memory, and she helped out with the chores around the house. Other than that, she was holed up in her room with her nose in a book. She knew that she was supposed to be applying for other jobs but- to be honest- she was terrified to leave the house. Meghan only got a thirty-day jail sentence on a misdemeanor charge, all because Kyra's anxiety had gotten the best of her. If she had just been able to keep her anxiety in check, then she wouldn't have blacked out and she would still have her memories.

Mrs. Walsh's temper had been very short over the past few days and Kyra knew it was her fault. Her mom thought that she was being lazy and that she needed to just 'get over it.' She knew that she needed to get on with her life but she wasn't quite ready to go back out into the real world. The only entry-level jobs that were even available in Cork, Oregon were in fast food, restaurants, retail, housekeeping, and mill work. Mill workers and loggers made really good money, but, since she was a girl (and of tiny stature), none of the mills would hire her. She just wanted a job where she could make more than minimum wage so she could afford to move out of her childhood home.

Kyra felt like she was at her wits end. *How could she apply for entry level jobs and expect to climb the ladder?* She had no college experience, and trade school was out of the question, so what now?...

It was the off season for the vineyards, so she highly doubted they'd be hiring right now. She could try applying at a couple of grocery stores, maybe even apply at a few of the hotels in the area. Maybe she could apply for a clerk position in a pharmacy? As a clerk, she'd be able to study and become a pharmacy technician.

That's it! That's exactly what she would do.

Kyra got her laptop out and spent the next four hours applying for every pharmacy in town, plus all of the surrounding areas. She even printed out several copies of her updated resumé. She didn't expect to hear back from any of them, but she was keeping her fingers crossed.

The smell of dinner wafted into Kyra's room, making her stomach growl loudly, reminding her that she hadn't eaten since breakfast that morning. She got up off her bed and went out to see if her mom needed help setting the table or with finishing dinner. When she walked into the dining room she saw that her family was sitting at the table and had already begun to eat.

What the hell? Why didn't they let me know that dinner was ready?...

"Nice of you to join us. Did you have a nice nap?" Mrs. Walsh asked her while rolling her eyes.

"What are you talking about? I wasn't napping, I was filling out job applications," Kyra said as she sat down at the table. Her brother and sister just sat there staring down at their plates, pushing their food around with their forks. What was everyone's problem today?

"Humph!" Mrs. Walsh let out a disgruntled sigh. "You seriously thought I'd buy that excuse?! If that were true, then where are all of these applications? Huh? You haven't left the house except to go to therapy, so how did you manage to get any applications? If you continue to lie, then you'll need to find somewhere else to live!" Kyra's mom was in serious need of a reality check.

"Bloody hell, mother! What decade do you think we live in? All applications are online these days! Get with the program. Sheesh! If you seriously don't believe me, then I'll get my computer out after dinner and you can check my browser history. Now, may I please have dinner? I haven't eaten since breakfast and I'm starving." Kyra knew that she shouldn't have talked to her mom like that, but she hadn't given her any reason to not trust her- especially not since her mother was able to come home to a spotless house today since Kyra had deep cleaned it earlier that morning right after Mrs. Walsh had left for work.

Kyra had suffered a trauma, so it's not like she'd be right back out there in the workforce after a couple of days or even weeks. Did her mom not realize how long the job process took these days? It's not like she could snap her fingers and get a job just like that. Especially when news spread like wildfire in their small town and no one wanted to hire someone that 'causes drama'. Most places that she had already applied to had taken

Meghan's side of the story before even giving her a chance.

"Fine, eat! But I already know you're lying!" Kyra had to bite her tongue and refrain from rolling her eyes. She had applied for six pharmacy jobs just today! And not just in Cork, but other nearby towns too. Yesterday she had applied at two different grocery stores. *What more did she expect her to do*?! The job market was down at the moment and a ton of people were currently unemployed. It's like her mom expected her to walk into each business and kiss their asses and beg for a job. At places where they didn't have any positions available, so why waste her time and theirs?

Kyra and her family sat there in silence as they ate their dinner. The whole time it was like Mrs. Walsh was trying to bore holes in Kyra's head. She glared through the *entire* meal. Her brother, Bryton, and Chloe cleared the table and went to the kitchen to do dishes.

Kyra's blood was boiling by this point, which was not good for her anxiety. Her hands were shaking and her heart was pounding in her chest. She HATED fighting with her parents, especially when she had done absolutely nothing wrong.

She knew she had nothing to feel guilty about, but her anxiety was telling her otherwise. It made her wonder if she had imagined the whole time she had spent applying for jobs for the past six hours. Now she was beginning to doubt and second guess herself. Had she spent too much time on one application? She knew that, to her mother, it would look like she had dozed off in the middle of an application if it took longer than ten minutes- even though a lot of applications now required aptitude tests on top of the initial application.

Thankfully, Kyra didn't have anything damning in her browser history, or else she would be going to her room to pack her bags right now instead of grabbing her laptop. She couldn't help but feel worried. She hadn't done anything wrong and she was always respectful to her mom, but for Mrs. Walsh to lose it like that at the dinner table, Kyra couldn't help but feel unwanted. Why did her mom seem to hate her so much? She realized that they did look very much alike- but could her mom seriously not realize that they were not the same person and that Kyra wasn't destined to make the same mistakes her mom had?

She knows that her mom has a full-time job as a nurse, but she usually never brought any of that stress home with her. Kyra hadn't told her mom about the pharmacy clerk applications because she knew that she would lecture her on how it's only minimum wage. She wanted to avoid any and all conflict, but she should've known that that would be asking for too much.

"Are you going to go get your laptop sometime this year? I don't have all damn night!" Mrs. Walsh obviously had some issue with her daughter, but for some reason she wouldn't tell Kyra what that issue was. It was so frustrating! Did her mom think she could read minds or something?

"I was on my way to get it. Chill out, mum! I don't know what your issue is, but if you aren't going to discuss it with me like an adult, then *please* stop with the attitude. I honestly can't handle it anymore! I don't need the extra stress right now. I'm doing the best I can! I am going to show you my browser history, but after that I am going to the library to study.

"Now, if you had given me a chance to talk before dinner, then you would've found out that I've decided to work my way up to a pharmacy technician because of all the times you mentioned about how the medical industry will always have job openings." Kyra's mom looked like a puppy that had been kicked. She immediately felt bad about how she had talked to her mother, but her mom had immensely overstepped. She didn't give in though to the narcissistic behavior or bring attention to it.

"You know what? Forget it! Just forget it. You should leave. I don't even want to look at you right now!" With that, Mrs. Walsh got up from the table, turned on her heel and stormed to her room, slamming the door. Kyra rolled her eyes and went to her room to start packing her bag. There was no way she was going to come back here after her study session at the library. She'd call some hotels before going in the library. Hopefully she could find a room on such short notice... Otherwise she'd be sleeping in her car tonight, which was not very safe with all of the drug addicts and homeless people hanging out around town. She did have a best friend she could stay with, but she didn't want to bring this negativity to him. He's already had to deal with enough of her family's shit to last a lifetime.

Rural areas of Oregon had really high drug use because there were plenty of secluded areas for meth labs to set up, which brought down the price for the local distribution- making it easily accessible. And the problem was only getting worse because there wasn't enough man power to fight the war on drugs. On top of all that, with the unemployment rate being so high, people were losing their homes and everything they own- and quite a few of them had resorted to drug use to escape their misery.

It sucked and Kyra wished there was something she could do to clean up the streets, but she was only one person... With all of the drug use, the crime rate was going through the roof. People were actually moving out of town and businesses were closing, which meant that the unemployment rate was getting higher. Her parents had told her that it was like 2007-2008 all over again. Soon Cork, Oregon would become a ghost town. Kyra wasn't very hopeful that she'd be able to get another job, but she was going to try and stay positive.

With her bags packed, Kyra left the house and loaded up her car. She wasn't sure when she'd be able to come back, but hopefully it'd be soon because she only had enough money to stay in a hotel for a week at most. Kyra had been saving up so she could fly back to Ireland and visit her grandmother for a couple of months next summer. The last time she went to visit was when she was eighteen and her whole family and her best friend had gone together. This time she wanted to go by herself. Her parents didn't like going to any of the castles because they had seen all of them 'a million times' when they were growing up. The only parts of Ireland that Kyra had been to were Dublin and Cork. Kyra had actually been born in Cork, Ireland.

While growing up in the States, people would get confused when she said she was born in Cork, but had immigrated to Oregon when she was four years old. It got irritating really fast, so she just told people that she was born in Ireland and would leave it at that. She'd swear her parents had moved them to Cork, Oregon because of their slight sense of humor and thought it would be punny.[3]

Kids were pretty cruel and would follow her around, calling her a leprechaun. Which was *extremely* insulting, but the kids didn't see it that way. Leprechauns weren't the 'cute little creatures' that hoarded gold at the end of the rainbow. They were actually evil and conniving- which she was *not*. Kyra had always been one of the nicest, purest souls anyone could meet but, with age, she had become bitter like Squidward on

Spongebob. That's why she never really had any friends while growing up.

There has only been one friend to stay by her side through the years and it was a miracle that they were still friends all these years later.

CHAPTER SIX

One good thing about Cork, Oregon- Kyra could drive any-where in less than ten minutes and that was *with* traffic. So, it didn't take her very long to get to the library. When she got there, she realized that they closed in less than an hour because of budget cutbacks.

Kyra hurried to look up all of the hotels' phone numbers. It took until the fourth call to find an available room. It was at a low star motel, but it was all she could afford. The phone calls took way longer than she thought they would, so she wouldn't be able to study at the library. Thankfully she still had enough time to go inside and borrow the books she needed.

While inside, she even asked for a job application because she had always wanted to be a librarian when she was a child. She constantly had her nose in a book, so why not?

Even though Cork only had about twenty thousand people, their library was *huge*! Kyra spent most of her spare time

24

there when she wasn't at work or taking care of her siblings while their parents were at work. As a child, she had always fantasized about living in a library like Belle- just without the Beast.

Kyra got back in her car and drove the half mile to the motel and got checked in. Thankfully, she was able to get an upstairs room so she wouldn't have to listen to people above her head all night while she was trying to study.

Once Kyra unloaded her bags and put them in her room, she went to the store down the street for some snacks and drinks. It was getting really chilly outside, so she was glad that she didn't have to sleep in her car tonight. It wasn't cold enough for her to get hypothermia, but it was cold enough to keep her up all night.

She could always call her best friend, Thomas, and stay with him but she didn't want to feel like a burden or make him feel like he *had* to let her move in. That would be very selfish and imposing of her. She didn't want to feel like a burden and eventually ruin the one and only friendship she had.

While Kyra was at the store, she couldn't think of what kind of food to eat. She didn't want to spend the rest of her money on just food. Since her motel room had a mini-fridge, Kyra was able to buy some yogurt and pre-cut fruit. Her go-to snacks for studying were yogurt, chocolate covered pretzels, and carrot sticks. Even though she didn't care for any of those things, she knew she needed brain food, especially now more than ever.

Kyra had a system for studying that had seemed to work very well for her all throughout school. She would study for about an hour, then take a ten-minute break and listen to music. That way, whatever subject she was studying would be associated with a song.

When Kyra was reached into the cooler for her yogurt, the hair on the back of her neck stood on end. She felt like someone was watching her. Turning around quickly revealed no one around her. Maybe she was just being paranoid, but this had been happening way too often lately. Every time she went to see her therapist, she would get that same feeling as she would walk from her car to the building.

Maybe it was just out of embarrassment about having to see a therapist in the first place, or because she was scared that Meghan would come after her again. She knew it made no sense since she wouldn't be getting released for about a week.

Kyra's gut was telling her to run away, to run as fast as she could. Maybe her anxiety and adrenaline were still out of whack from her fight with her mom. Once again, she shook off the feeling and went to pay for her things. Thankfully, she had been able to park right in front of the store and she was able to throw her things in and take off.

Kyra drove back to the motel and locked herself in her room. She immediately closed the curtains tight and turned on some music before putting her food away. She heard someone in the room next to hers open and close their door. After a few minutes, she was able to relax and got her books out to study.

It was about two in the morning and Kyra was so exhausted that she fell asleep on her notes. She had been studying for the past six hours, which was three times longer than she had ever been able to stay focused before.

Sometime around eleven, she had moved from the desk to the bed to study, so she was very surprised she was able to stay awake for so long. Kyra had only gotten about four hours of sleep per night since the "incident" because she kept having nightmares, but she forgot what they were about the second her eyes would open. Three weeks had gone by but she *still* had no memory of what had happened. She did find out that Meghan was only going to be getting thirty days in jail, unless Kyra's memories miraculously came back within the next week.

If her memories were to come back, then there would be a trial and Meghan could be looking at the next *five years* in prison- minimum. Even though she couldn't remember the incident, she could still remember all of the previous altercations with Meghan. In her opinion, Meghan deserved *way* more than thirty days or five years. She was a danger to society.

Before the incident, Kyra had secretly been planning to move back to Ireland and live with her grandmother. It wasn't for sure yet, but she had been weighing the pros and cons of moving for quite some time now- almost since the day she graduated from high school. The only things keeping her in the States were money, her anxiety, her siblings, and her best friend.

Just the thought of moving halfway around the world and leaving her family behind to live with a grandmother she barely knew, terrified her to no end. Her mom's mom was really sweet and down to earth, but Kyra didn't know of anything that they had in common. Plus, how would she even be able to get a job once she had moved?! Her parents hadn't taught her or her siblings very much of the Irish language, so that's just one more thing to worry about. Thankfully English is widely spoken, or she'd be totally screwed. She'd feel unwelcome no matter where she decided to live.

She felt like an impostor... Not an impostor, more of an outsider than anything. Was she Irish, or was she an American? She didn't seem to fit in anywhere and it made her feel adrift in life. It made it hard for her to envision what she wanted her future to look like because she had no sense of self. Maybe all her studying will pay off and maybe once she gets some distance from her mother, maybe she'll finally be able to begin to figure out who she is as a person.

CHAPTER SEVEN

Kyra woke up the next day and couldn't remember where she was and immediately began to panic. After several *very* long minutes, events from the day before came flooding back. She reached for her phone and jumped out of bed, in a panic once again. It was two in the afternoon and she had about ten missed calls from her mom and almost as many voicemails. She listened to the first couple of calls thinking that someone was seriously hurt.

The more voicemails she listened to, the more irritated and annoyed she became. Her mom was wondering why she wasn't home when she got up for work. Was she serious?! Mrs. Walsh had kicked her out, telling her to leave. How was Kyra supposed to know what time she would be allowed back in the house? Her mom made it clear that she wanted her gone for more than a few hours.

Kyra took a deep breath and practiced what she was going

29

to say when she called her mom back. Whenever she dreaded a phone call, Kyra would brush her teeth, go to the bathroom, then get dressed up as if the person on the other end of the call could tell if her breath stank or if she were stark naked. It was something she had learned to do to help ease her anxiety, as all of those tasks helped to calm her and allow her heart rate to stabilize.

"Okay... Here goes nothing," Kyra muttered to herself, sighing as she called her mother.

Ring, ring! Ring, ring!

The call went to voicemail after only a couple of rings, so she figured her mom was at work because that was the only time she would not answer her phone.

"Hey, mum. I'm okay. I stayed the night at a motel since I was up late studying. I'll be home for dinner so we can talk. I love you, bye." Kyra hung up and sucked in a deep breath, not realizing she had been holding her breath the whole time. She was shaking so badly that she had to lay back down.

To occupy her mind, she began counting the stripes on the curtains and then the ceiling tiles. Then she started packing up her notes and getting them organized in the folder that she bought from the dollar store. She decided that she would be better off to go ahead and check out because she really needed to try and save as much money as possible and didn't want to be charged for a second night. She grabbed her bags and went downstairs to get checked out.

Kyra knew she'd beat her mom home, so she would just hide in her room as soon as she got to the house. Her room had always felt like a safe place, like no one could hurt her as long as she was in her room.

There wasn't anyone in line in the main office, so she was able to check out quickly. A few moments later, Kyra was loaded up in her car and on her way home. She got stuck behind a train, so instead of it only taking five minutes to get home, it ended up taking twenty minutes. There was a mill at the North end of town so the train would stop on the tracks for a while as it got loaded up. It usually happened around the same time every day, but she hadn't been paying much attention to the time as she was anxious about going back home.

She wasn't planning on unpacking when she got home because, knowing her mom, she'd be kicked out again- possibly voluntarily. Her mom always treated her as if she were a lazy, good for nothing slob. Which makes no sense as she always kept her room impeccably clean and was the one who did all of the chores around the house.

As a nurse, her mom had seen *plenty* of people with mental illnesses, but when it came to her own daughter, Kyra was an 'attention seeker.' Like, what?! How was hiding out in her room, or throwing herself into her work be her seeking attention? Kyra *had* had several anxiety attacks while in public and people stared, but it's not like she had done it on purpose! It was humiliating when people stared at her like they wished she'd disappear. Which is exactly what she wished would happen in those moments- to just disappear and cease to exist.

Sometimes Kyra felt as if she were losing her mind because she would be perfectly fine one second, then a total mess the next. She would even get really sharp pains in her head that would sometimes last for a couple of days. She had even brought it up to her mom on several occasions, but she would brush it off, claiming that Kyra was just stressed or that she was being dramatic. Kyra was hoping that was true, but her gut said otherwise. Normally, she'd do a lot of research on it, but she knew that nothing good would come of it. Looking up her symptoms online would only freak her out more by adding to her stress and anxiety level. 'Curiosity killed the cat' as the saying goes.

Kyra pulled into the driveway behind her father's car and sat there, working up the courage to go inside. Her and her father always got along and had a lot in common, but he tended to be a little cold and distant. It made her Kyra feel like there was something majorly wrong with her that made both of her parents want nothing to do with her.

Most of her childhood, her father would be away on business for long stretches of time. He wasn't big on confrontations either, so Kyra knew he wouldn't say anything when she walked in or that he would say anything to her mother once she got home. Her father was the only person in her family who didn't treat her like she was crazy, or claim she was seeking attention. She had a feeling that he had anxiety too and that's why he was so distant, but she had no way of proving it.

She couldn't ask him about it either because he would be offended by her asking such a personal question. They were never close enough for that kind of discussion- which made her feel even more unwanted.

Even though Kyra was an adult and couldn't be grounded, she snuck into the house, stomach in knots and her palms all sweaty. She was able to make it to her room upstairs without being noticed. They had a lot of creaky stairs so it was a surprise that no one came looking to see who was upstairs.

When she had walked in the front door, she could smell something good. Kyra assumed it was her dad's turn to make dinner because it smelled like beef stew, which was making her mouth water. He made it whenever the weather was dreary and chilly like today. He always said it reminded him of his childhood home back in Ireland. She wanted to go back downstairs to help with dinner, but she didn't want to see her mom the second she got home from work. Maybe once her mom had showered and gotten her comfy clothes on, then Kyra would venture out of her room.

Kyra hadn't even been home for ten minutes when she heard her mom's car pull into the driveway. She didn't dare peak out the window though, which was clearly pointless. Her car was in the driveway so, obviously, her mom already knew she was home. She was hoping that- since she got home before her mom- it would give her a couple of brownie points.

Kyra decided to clean and reorganize her already clean room while she waited for her mom to get cleaned up. She actually wanted to start packing up her room, but she had nowhere else to go. Definitely not somewhere that was free. Plus, if she packed anything, her mom would *definitely* notice right away.

Knock, knock.

"Come in!" Kyra said as she was putting her last few books away.

"Kyra, can we talk before dinner?" Mrs. Walsh asked with a stony look on her face, her lips in a thin line.

"Sure. What did you have on your mind?"

"Not here. Let's go sit at the table. There are too many *distractions* in here." With that, her mom left her room with Kyra following behind reluctantly. Apparently, blank walls void of any pictures or posters and a room with next to nothing in it was a "distraction." They sat down across from each other at the table in complete silence for several minutes.

"Look, Kyra. To be honest, your attitude has gotten on my last nerve. I constantly have to tell you to do your chores and about applying for jobs. All you've been doing it moping around the house for weeks. You're so bloody lazy! I'm sick and tired of it!" Mrs. Walsh declared, with her nose up in the air.

What in the actual hell was her mother going on about now? That is literally the complete opposite from what she's been doing since the incident happened.

"Bloody hell! Who the hell do you think takes care of the kids when you and dad are at work?! Who do you think cleans the house or does the laundry? Huh? Yet I still have time to help the kids with their homework *and* apply for jobs when everyone else has gone to bed. I manage to do all of that on only four hours of sleep every single night!

"Not ONCE have you asked me how I was doing since the incident! If you had asked, you would know that I have nightmares all night long, and during the day I'm terrified that Meghan is going to finish what she started. Did you know that she gets out of jail at the end of next week?" Kyra sat there shaking, her stomach in knots, and her palms sweaty. She felt like her heart was about to beat out of her chest.

"I know you're scared, Kyra... I'm scared too, but that doesn't mean you should give up! Who cares about Meghan?! Both of you need to grow up. I know that's not what you want to hear right now, but I don't care.

"Growing up is hard, but that's just a part of life. Some days you might be knocked flat on your arse, and other days you'll feel like you're on cloud nine. That's just how life goes. Once you realize that, you'll feel better! So, stop moping around and hiding out in your room all the time!" Kyra looked at her mom sitting across from her and felt something snap inside of her. The beast had broken out of the cage and there was no way to coax it back inside. She couldn't keep her mouth shut any longer...

"I already know that! I know my luck is bound to take a turn for the better, but lately it's just been one damn thing after another. I've had days where I honestly didn't know how I'd be able to keep going," Kyra yelled at her mom as tears were falling down her face. She could taste her tears as they fell into her mouth. Kyra continued with a shaky voice, "On those days, I tried to take my own life... At the last second I would remind myself of all the people I'd be leaving behind and of all the possibilities for the future.

"Every single day is an uphill battle. Depression isn't something that goes away on its own. It's not something you can just ignore either, because ignoring it can actually do more harm than good. You need to understand that there's nothing 'wrong' with me for having anxiety either. Mental disorders aren't a joke, they're also not a disability. Yes, I may not like doing things outside of my comfort zone, or like sticking to a routine, but *that's* how I deal with my mental illnesses!" Nearly out of breath, Kyra started feeling a pit forming in her stomach. The anxiety attack was coming and there was nothing she could do about it.

"Kyra! That's no way to live! That's coping, not living- *coping*. Maybe if you found a hobby, something that you really enjoy, you'd be happy and feel better. Being so uptight all the time isn't good for you! Go do something fun and, oh, I don't know, maybe make some new friends in the process." She shrugged her shoulders and continued to sit there like she had the answers to all the world's problems.

"*Máthair*! That's not how it works!" Kyra screamed. She closed her eyes and took a deep breath. Once she collected her thoughts, she looked at her mom and tried to keep her cool. "I can't just DO something that's out of my comfort zone. Doing things spur of the moment can cause me to have a panic attack so severe that I become physically ill. You know this, you've seen it for yourself! Your comments about me needing to 'just calm down' don't help either, they just make it worse.

"I love you, mum, but you need to respect that I have boundaries and that there are some things you need to keep to yourself. Comments about my appetite or my appearance also don't help. I know that I've put on some weight, but that's not for you to judge. I'm not you, and that's okay! I'm on my own path and I need to see where it takes me. And honestly, mother, when the *fuck* do you think I'd have the time for a hobby when you seem to think I'm your fucking nanny and not your daughter?" They sat there, both crying and glaring at each other.

"I think it would be best if I went to stay with a friend for a few days. We're clearly not getting anywhere here and we both need to take time to cool down. I don't want to make papa and the kids upset, because then we'll all be mad at each other and nothing good will come of it. If I plan on staying for more than a few days, I'll text you and let you know." With that, Kyra got up from the table and left the house. She got in her car and texted her friend, Thomas, letting him know she was on her way. Kyra started her car and quickly backed out of the driveway, nearly hitting their neighbor's car in her rush.

Even though she was only driving a few streets over, she turned on her relaxing playlist because she decided to drive around for a while until she calmed down. Even she knew she was not in the right head space to be behind the wheel and that the best thing to do would be to go straight to Thomas's house, but she wasn't quite ready to talk to anyone about what had just happened.

By the time she had calmed down, Kyra realized she had no clue where she was. None of the road names sounded familiar, so she pulled off the road into someone's long driveway and turned on her GPS. It was an older model so it took a couple of minutes to calculate. It would have been much faster to just use the maps function on her phone, but she was in a dead zone- which meant she was way outside of town at that point.

It had been raining during her drive and it was starting to get dark out. She had probably another fifteen minutes or so until it got dark and she had always had a hard time driving in the dark because she would get disoriented. It also didn't help that she was going to need new windshield wipers soon. They left streaks of water every time they made a pass across the windshield, making it little bit harder to see while driving.

When the GPS finished calculating, Kyra put in Thomas's address just to see how far off she was. The directions popped right up and Kyra's stomach twisted. She was *twenty-five miles* in the wrong direction in the middle of nowhere... How did she not realize she was going the wrong direction? How did she not even realize she was no longer in town? And how the hell had she driven *so far* without noticing?!

Kyra texted Thomas back and told him that she was just going to spend the night at a hotel and would update him in the morning. She knew it wouldn't send until she was able to get to a spot with cell service, but she didn't worry about it. Kyra took a deep breath and turned her car back around. She still had plenty of time to get back to the familiarity of town before dark, but she still didn't want to drive too fast.

She had only driven about fifty feet when she saw movement

out of the corner of her eye. She turned her head, looking out the passenger window, seeing a flash of headlights. She didn't have time to react when she heard the sound of grinding metal and felt the force of the impact...

The sound of grinding metal was so loud that all Kyra's brain could register was that she was upside down. The other vehicle had hit her with so much force that her car had flipped upside down into the ditch on the other side of the road. Her vision was blurry and her brain was foggy. Her body was starting to go into shock, so she couldn't feel the pain from her broken bones or the cold wind that was whipping around her. She could smell blood and lots of it, but she couldn't tell where it was coming from. The sound of crunching glass alerted her to someone standing next to her.

There was a sudden, white-hot pain as the person bent down and cut her seat belt in one swift motion. Her head never hit the ground but she could have been wrong about that because of how badly her head was pounding. The new pain in her neck wasn't helping either.

They dragged her out of the wreckage and laid her down on the side of the road, then walked away. She tried calling for help, but the shock and pain had drained all of her energy. Was this the other driver helping her out of guilt, or had there been someone else driving by that had seen the accident and stopped to help?

The person came back and started tending to her injuries, which cause Kyra to scream as they were stabilizing her broken leg. Her scream felt like it was coming from the depths of her soul. The pain was so immense that Kyra immediately lost consciousness, but not before she caught a glimpse of a familiar set of eyes.

CHAPTER EIGHT

When Kyra came to, she was completely disoriented. She had no clue what time it was, or if it was day or night. The only thing she knew for certain was that she had been in a car accident- her pain was proof of that. Someone had gotten her out of the car, and now she was in what looked like a barn. There was a faint smell of hay but there was another smell that was overpowering that she couldn't quite put her finger on.

Kyra tried to stand, but pain shot up and down her left side and she collapsed back to the ground. All of the bones had either been broken or fractured from the accident from her head down to her ankle- that was when the fear really started setting in. She was so overwhelmed by pain that she began to fade in and out of consciousness.

When she woke up, she had been strapped to a chair and wrapped in chains. How long had she been out? Minutes? Hours? *Days*?! That part was uncertain. What she was certain about was that the chains were very cold and the chair looked like it had seen better days. There were grooves in the armrests-like someone else had been chained to it once before.

Kyra looked around as her vision began to clear. There were fluorescent lights hanging from the ceiling and Kyra could see the dust from the hay and dirt floating in the air. The lights looked out of place for a barn. They looked kind of like the type of lights you'd see in an office building or a school. She had always imagined a barn would have those big, round lights that hang down from the ceiling- the ones that would sway when a breeze would blow through the barn.

There was a movement in the shadows and Kyra had to swallow back a scream. There was no way she was about to show her kidnapper any sign of weakness. Kyra began to struggle against her restraints to see if she could slip out of them- that was when she realized that she no longer had any broken bones. Had she imagined it all?...

No. That kind of pain is not something she could imagine. Had it possibly been *months* since the accident?! That was the only possible logical explanation her brain could conjure up. Injuries as bad as hers couldn't heal like that in just a matter of days, or even a week.

A man dressed in all black stepped out of the shadows and stood there staring at her. Her senses were telling her to run, but she was chained to the chair too tightly to break free, so she quit struggling and glared at him instead. The longer she looked at him, she'd swear she had seen him before. There was a memory nagging at the back of her mind, but it was still too fuzzy to remember.

"What the bloody hell do you want from me?! Where am I? How long have I been here? How did I get here?" Kyra pestered him with questions. He didn't answer, just continued to stare. "Answer me you son of a bitch! What is your deal?!" All of a sudden he was right in her face. All she did was blink and he was somehow able to move over twenty feet in less than a second.

She felt the hairs on the back of her neck go up as her body responded to the obvious threat. Her subconscious responded in fear, but her conscious mind was still focused on how familiar he looked. It was the eyes that kept drawing her attention and poking at a distant memory that was still too foggy to remember.

"Your car broke down, so you had to hitchhike back to town. You won't remember anything from the past couple days," the guy stated as he stared into Kyra's eyes.

"What the bloody hell are you talking about?! None of that happened, you psychotic bastard! You can bet that once I get out of here I'll be pressing charges!" Kyra screamed in his face. Her heart was racing and her breathing was shallow and fast, as if she were about to hyperventilate.

"What makes you think you'll make it out alive?" The guy asked with a creepy grin on his face. Chills ran down her spine and she closed her eyes. Kyra tried to focus on the sound of the rain hitting the barn roof as she tried to get her heart rate back to normal. When she opened her eyes and her eyes met his, it hit her. He was the paramedic that saw to her after the incident...

"I think that if you had really wanted to kill me, you would've done it already. You could have killed me in the ambulance weeks ago. So, what do you want from me? What do you want you sick, sadistic bastard?!"

"The correction question is, 'What can you do for me, you

sick, sadistic bastard?'" Kyra's mind was still a little fuzzy, so she wasn't sure what it was he was trying to say.

"What are you talking about? That's what I just asked you!" Kyra exclaimed.

"Okay, I guess I'll have to spell it out for you then. I can give you anything you want. I've been watching you for quite some time, and the whole time I've seen you do nothing but struggle. When I noticed you always with your nose in the *Twilight* books, I figured out a way to help you. The hard part was trying to figure out if it was something you *truly* wanted. Since you woke up, have you wondered at all about your broken bones? Even now, you can feel your mind become clearer by the minute."

"What-what have you done to me?!" She asked, staring up at him in pure horror.

"You *really* need to ask? Come on now, I thought you were a lot smarter than that, Kyra. Really think about it. You're a vampire now! You never have to sleep again, you're much stronger physically, *and* you can go out during the day. Don't you get it, Kyra?! I've helped you by making you better!"

Kyra just sat there, stunned, not moving. She stared at him like he was a raving lunatic. He was giving off an Evan Peters from *American Horror Story* vibe and Kyra was terrified. He looked like someone that was- or had been previously- in the military. He had the sharp haircut, the clean-shaven face, and the overall slim, muscular stature. He wasn't short either. She'd guess that he was about six-foot one, maybe six-foot two.

"What's your name? Shouldn't I know the name of the man who made me?" She tried to come off as convincing as possible.

"It's Jack, Jack Hastings. I don't know if you remember, but we actually went to school together until junior year. Everyone thought I moved away, but that was actually when I was turned. My car broke down on my way home from my part-time job. I was actually just down the road from here when I was attacked. I should've just stayed in my car and called for help instead of trying to walk home. After I was attacked, I crawled here into the barn and this is where I turned. That's how I came up with the idea to run you off the road. Almost like history coming full circle." He had a distant look in his eyes the more he spoke.

"Jack, I'm so sorry that happened to you, but what made you think that I couldn't decide if I wanted this for myself or not? You took away my free will by turning me without my permission. Now I'm cursed for all eternity and I can *never* go back. I can't have children now, which is something I've always wanted. You would have known that if you had actually came up to me and given me the option. I can't even go back home now either! What if I hurt my family?! I'd never be able to live with myself after something like that. Speaking of my family, they'll be wondering what happened to me." Kyra began frantically looking around for her phone that she realized was no longer in her pocket. Had she lost it in the accident?

"There's nothing to worry about. I took your phone while you were unconscious and texted your mom saying that you needed a couple more days away. In the meantime, I'll be teaching you how to control your urges, and a few tricks that we can do. If you want to be able to fit in society and not get caught, you'll need to learn how to do everything at human speed again. It took nearly a year to be able to control myself, but I have a feeling that you'll adjust a lot faster."

Kyra was still trying to process all of the new, life altering information that she didn't notice that something about her was different. It was like something was nagging in the back of her mind, but she couldn't quite put her finger on it.

"So, can you smell when a woman is on her period?..." Kyra asked as her face turned nearly as red as her hair. She was trying to make idle conversation to give her brain a chance to catch up and possibly come up with a plan to escape. "That's something I've always wondered about... I haven't read a single vampire book that mentioned anything about it."

"Yes, but it doesn't smell very good..." He said as he grimaced. "It's equivalent to a human walking past someone with really bad body odor. It's very off putting. So, do you have any other questions? If not, then we should really be getting started on your training. Before we get started, I need to run to the house to get some blood bags. You need to feed to build your strength." With that said, Jack disappeared. Kyra was still chained to the chair, so she used the time alone to process her thoughts. *So much for trying to distract him,* she thought flippantly.

It was in those few shorts moments that Kyra realized what was different about herself. Her anxiety was gone. Just... gone! How was that even possible?! It shouldn't be possible...should it? She'd had anxiety since she was twelve, possibly even before that. She couldn't remember a time when she didn't feel on edge, or like she was going to jump out of her skin.

"Hey, Kyra, are you alright? You look pale, even for you. Did something happen while I was gone?" Jack asked as he walked into the barn. He set the blood bags down on one of the tables and walked over to her, bending down to be at eye level with her. "Did your memories come back?" He asked, his eyes full of concern.

"My anxiety... It's gone... Jack, it's gone!" Kyra exclaimed as she burst into tears. She knew that that was the last thing she should be worrying about when what she really needed was to find a way out of here.

"I don't know what or how it happened, but it's completely gone! Can you believe it?! Can you unchain me, please? We need to celebrate!" She said with a huge grin on her face. Jack undid the chains, but had a somber look on his face the entire time.

"Kyra... There's another reason why I turned you... I wasn't sure it would work, but it clearly did. When you were in the hospital, I was there because I wanted to make sure you were okay. When your mom went to get the doctor, I overheard them talking about the results from you MRI. Kyra... You had a brain tumor. Where it was, the doctor said it was more than likely benign. That was creating a chemical imbalance and that's what was causing your anxiety." Jack looked like he was about to cry. How could Kyra possibly be mad at him now? He had saved her life in more ways than one...

"So, my mum knew this whole time and kept it from me? Why would she do that? She's a nurse for crying out loud! She had *NO* right to make that decision! I'm almost twenty-two for crying out loud!" Kyra was so angry that she started seeing red.

How could her mom be so selfish?! There *HAD* to be more to the story that neither of them knew about... Kyra closed her eyes and took slow, deep breaths to calm herself down. She focused on her breaths and the beating of her heart. She tapped her fingers to the rhythm of her heart while keeping her eyes closed.

After a few minutes, she opened her eyes to see Jack gaping at her in utter shock. "What are you staring at?" She asked him.

"How the hell did you do that?! I've never seen a new vampire be able to control themselves like that!"

"Maybe I don't like being upset or angry. Did you think about that? Maybe it's from all the years of having to keep my emotions in check because of my anxiety. Any kind of stress always made it way worse. I guess I've just had plenty of practice," Kyra said, shrugging her shoulders.

"I guess so… If so, you may not need very much training. First things first though. You need to feed, then you need to see yourself in a mirror. If you can keep calm after your first feeding, then we can move from the barn to the house where you'll be much more comfortable." He ushered her back to the chair and handed her a blood bag.

Kyra was nervous because she had always hated the sight of blood. It would make her queasy and feel faint, which was ridiculous because she was a woman, so you'd think it wouldn't bother her anymore. She could smell the sweet, iron aroma coming from the blood and nearly lost her stomach.

Kyra closed her eyes and took a deep breath before pouring some blood in her mouth. It hit her tongue and suddenly every nerve in her body came to life. It was better than an orgasm in her opinion. And yes, she knew what that was. She wasn't completely innocent in this life.

The only way she'd be able to explain it would be as if she had been out in the cold all day, then went inside for a hot cup of tea- like warmth was spreading through her veins. She drained the whole bag and basked in the buzzing warmth. She asked Jack for another bag but, when he didn't respond, she opened her eyes. He was watching her with a dazed look on his face.

"What now, Jack? You're killing my buzz," she huffed as she crossed her arms in front of her self-consciously.

"You really need to look in a mirror now that your transition is complete… When we turn, our eyes change color depending on what kind of person we are- or so I've been told. We also become more attractive as a way to draw in our 'prey.' Everything about our appearances becomes more vibrant. Come on, let's head up to the house, you- you'll see what I mean," he stammered.

Jack grabbed her hand and led her out of the barn and up the hill to the house.

CHAPTER NINE

Even though it was the middle of the night, Kyra could make out every single detail around her. From the peeling paint on the barn siding, to the drops of frosty dew on the grass. She could hear a group of deer munching on the grass nearly a mile away. It sounded as if she were right there next to them. She could also hear the nearby creek and the nocturnal animals lapping up the water.

Kyra wanted to stop and look at everything, but Jack kept pulling her up the hill to the farmhouse. When she saw the house, she couldn't help but gasp. It was one of the most beautiful houses she had ever seen! There was a big wrap-around deck with a cozy porch swing that she could imagine herself sitting on while sipping a hot cup of tea on a rainy day.

When they walked into the house, they were in what looked like a mudroom and they took off their shoes and replaced them for a pair of house slippers. They went to the living room and Kyra's jaw nearly hit the floor. The room was *massive*! There was a huge, rustic stone fireplace on one wall with giant windows on either side. Kyra had a feeling that she would be spending a lot of time in this house…

Jack led her down the hallway to the bathroom, turning the light on and ushering her inside. There was a huge, claw footed tub, but next to that tub was a full-length mirror. She met her gaze in the mirror and gasped… Her eyes were such a brilliant, light green that it appeared as if they were glowing.

Upon closer inspection, she could see that her eyes had little brown speckles, which matched the freckles on her face. Her hair turned a darker red, but was so vibrant and bright that, from a distance, it would look as is her head were on fire. Her hair reminded her of Merida from the kid's movie *Brave*. She looked down at her clothes, which were filthy and covered in her own blood. One thing caught her eye when she looked at her jeans.

"Wait a second… Did I get taller too?!" Kyra asked in wonder, not looking away from her reflection. Her favorite jeans were now two inches too short.

"I guess so," he chuckled. "Well, I'll let you get cleaned up. There's stuff in the cabinets, use whatever you like, and there's a clean robe on the back of the door. Your bags are in the bedroom across the hall. I unloaded your car after I hauled it back here. I'm going to go start making dinner, so take your time." With that, he backed out of the bathroom, closing the door behind him. Kyra stood in the middle of the bathroom for a few minutes while she let everything soak in.

She had to be hallucinating… *right*?

Kyra snapped out of it and started rummaging through the cabinets. There was a wide selection of women's products, but she wasn't going to think about the reasoning behind that right now. She grabbed the first bottles she saw because all she could think about at that moment was getting clean. She was beginning to smell like a rotting corpse and it was making her stomach roll. Kyra turned on the tub and brushed her teeth while she waited for it to fill up. Just the simple act of brushing her teeth made her feel so much better.

The tub was taking too long, so Kyra jumped in and sat in the few measly inches of warm water. She couldn't think of when the last time she bathed was. Maybe that one afternoon at the motel? Shrugging her shoulders, Kyra submerged herself in the water so she could get her hair wet. It was so quiet and peaceful under the water. Kyra closed her eyes and let herself enjoy a few moments of complete silence. She didn't feel tired, it was more like mental exhaustion, as if she had been up all-night studying.

When Kyra finished bathing, she got out of the tub, walked across the bathroom, and put the robe on. She had left some conditioner in her hair in the hopes that the brush wouldn't get stuck in her thick, red curls. Kyra had always loved brushing her hair- she couldn't explain it, but it always relaxed her. There was a knock on the bathroom door and Kyra jumped. She had been completely immersed in her own little world.

"Hey Kyra, are you okay in there? You've been in there for over an hour…" Jack said through the door, his voice full of concern.

"I'm fine, I just needed to relax. You can come in," Kyra replied. Jack opened the door, but stayed in the doorway. "I'm sorry if dinner got cold, I honestly just needed some time to myself. I can't even remember the last time I was so relaxed…" Kyra said as she continued to brush her hair.

"That's alright, I completely understand," he said as he watched the brush running through her hair. "I made beef stew. It's on the stove whenever you're ready to eat," he said and started to leave.

"Wait! We can eat human food?" She asked. She had completely forgotten to ask about that earlier.

"Of course! It's not very realistic to be able to live off of blood alone. And yes, you still have to go to the bathroom too." He chuckled and left the bathroom. Kyra stood there watching Jack walk away. He moved so silently that, with Kyra's new enhanced sense of hearing, she could only hear the slight sound of fabric brushing together. It unnerved her a little, but that was something she'd have to adjust to. She was curious to see how loud humans were.

Setting the hairbrush down on the bathroom vanity, Kyra walked across the hall to get dressed. Jack had been kind enough to unpack her clothes and lay them out so they wouldn't be a wrinkled mess. She grabbed her favorite emerald green sweater and her dark denim jeans and put them on. Grabbing her matching green scrunchie, she put her hair up in a messy bun as she walked back down the hall to the kitchen to find Jack.

"Well, you've definitely got the whole human speed thing down. I was beginning to think that maybe you were still human," Jack joked, walking up behind her. "How are you feeling? You look a little out of it..."

"I *feel* out of it. Almost like I'm floating, like I'm dreaming. There's *no way* this is reality! Things like this just don't happen to me..." Kyra closed her eyes and slapped her face as hard as she could. *Shit, that hurt!* She thought to herself. She opened her eyes and saw Jack in front of her. "Well, looks like I'm not dreaming..." She said, sighing.

"Are you okay? That was a pretty hard slap..." Jack asked as he reached his arm out, cupping her cheek in his hand.

"I'm fine," she said, taking a step back, letting his arm fall back to his side. "Look, I appreciate what you've done for me, but you need to know that that doesn't mean I have feelings for you. The only way I could *possibly* feel anything for you is if I trusted you. You broke that trust when you turned me against my will. It's going to take a lot of work and time for you to ever regain my trust," Kyra told him, crossing her arms in front of her, trying to look serious. Jack looked taken aback and baffled, like he couldn't wrap his mind around what she said.

"Kyra, I am *so* sorry! But I'm not going to say I'd take it back if I could, because that would be a lie," he said, grabbing her hand in both of his. "I'm *glad* I turned you and I harbor zero regrets. I couldn't stand to see you so miserable for even a second longer. It broke my heart that day when I got a call that a young woman was unconscious in a restaurant parking lot. The moment I saw your bright red hair and smelled the blood from your wounds, I thought I was too late. In the span of a few seconds, I realized that I have no future without you in it. I love you, Kyra..."

Kyra was completely speechless. His declaration of love did nothing to change her mind, but she didn't want to scare him off and have to try and fend for herself. She was so stressed that she began to hyperventilate.

"Kyra, breathe... It's okay. I don't expect you to say anything back, I just needed you to know how I feel. I didn't want you to constantly feel uncomfortable around me and feel like you need to walk on egg shells all the time. If you never feel the same way about me, that's okay! My heart may be broken for a little while, but that's okay, that's on me. No matter what though, I still want to be a part of your life." Jack averted his eyes and let go of her hand.

Were there really men in the world that thought that way? She thought those kind of men only existed in books and that's because those books were created by women.

"Look, I appreciate you telling me, but I need to focus on myself. I can't afford to be distracted right now. I've spent so much time being the person that my mum wanted me to be that I haven't had a chance to figure it out for myself. What if I'm not actually nice? What if I'm extremely self-centered? Do you think it would be fair of me to give you a chance when I don't even know who I really am?" Kyra asked. "Maybe someday there could be a chance for us, but only once I've come to terms with my new reality." Kyra gave Jack a friendly hug, but she couldn't deny how right it felt being in his arms.

"So, are you ready for dinner? I made something to go with the stew," he questioned as he let go of her and walked over to the oven. "How do you feel about cornbread?" He asked.

"*Cornbread*?! You made cornbread?! I hope you weren't expecting to eat any because I can literally eat the whole pan by myself," she chuckled nervously. The smell of the stew mixed with the aroma of warm cornbread was making her stomach growl.

"When I was growing up, cornbread was always one of my favorite things to eat on a cold day. But it also made me feel a little better, so I thought maybe it would be the same for you," he shrugged. He dished both of them up a bowl of stew and sat down at the breakfast bar. Kyra was so hungry that she would've gladly eaten straight from the pot. Which wasn't all that surprising since Kyra hadn't had human food in nearly four days. Well, she assumed it had been four days, if she were to go off of the calendar that he had hanging up on the fridge.

They sat in silence while they ate. It wasn't an awkward silence, more of a content type of silence. Kyra looked out the window and could see that dawn was fast approaching. This would be the first time in a long time that she'd be able to see the sunrise. But this time would be different in so many ways, beginning with the fact that this would be just one of the endless number of sunrises of her now immortal life. She couldn't wait to see the beauty of another day.

CHAPTER TEN

Kyra made a pot of chamomile tea before heading out of the house to sit on the porch swing. As she waited for the sun to come up, she closed her eyes and listened to the sounds of the approaching dawn. The cattle out in the pastures were snorting and rustling around as if they were celebrating that they were lucky enough to see another day. She could hear the trickle of water from a nearby stream and the birds chirping in the trees.

"May I join you?"

Kyra looked up to see Jack standing there with a cup of coffee. She nodded and closed her eyes again. It was so peaceful that Kyra felt as if she were transported to another realm. If she focused hard enough, it was as if time had slowed down- even though she knew it was only because her brain could now process information twenty times faster, but that didn't make it any less relaxing.

"Is it like this every morning?" She asked as she opened her eyes. The sun was just about to peak above the mountain. This was absolute paradise to her. It was so cold out that the steam coming off their drinks looked like little white clouds, as did each of their breaths.

"Just about- even on rainy days. Just wait until it starts to snow next month, then you'll know true peace. The snow makes the sound completely disappear. It's just a deafening silence which is a nice change once you've spent a lot of time in the human world," Jack told her.

They continued to sit in silence as the world woke up around them. Kyra could imagine how quiet it would be with a blanket of fluffy, white snow. She had always wanted to build an igloo, but they never got enough snow to be able to do anything like that. They did get a large amount back in February, but Kyra had been too busy taking care of her siblings to actually enjoy the snow. They had gotten so much snow that the whole area had lost power for three days and the surrounding rural areas had been without power for something like fifteen days.

Thinking about the snow made her think of her brother and sister. She missed them so much! But she didn't trust herself to be around them, and she had no clue how long it would be before she could see them again. Hopefully she could within the next week, but she highly doubted it. She hadn't been around any humans yet so she couldn't say for sure how she'd react.

"Kyra, look," Jack nudged her, distracting her from her thoughts. When she looked up, the sky was a very faint pink and the light rays from the sun began to light up the valley. She had never seen anything so beautiful in her entire life... There were so many vibrant colors all around her that it took a long time for her to take everything in. The thousands of trees surrounding the valley had bursts of orange, red, and yellow scattered among the pine and Douglas Fir trees. There were a few trees in town that were always a bright, vibrant yellow. She could only imagine what they would look like with her new, enhanced vision.

"Wow... Just wow..." That's all Kyra could manage to say because there were honestly no words in her vocabulary that were good enough to describe what she was seeing. If humans could see what she was seeing, she was fairly certain that pollution would become a thing of the past. There was no way that anyone who saw what she was seeing would have a single thought of destruction running through their minds.

"Would you like to meet everyone else?" Jack asked. Kyra looked at him so fast that a human wouldn't have been able to see it.

"What do you mean by everyone else?! I thought we were alone?" She questioned him.

"Did you think I could take care of the whole ranch, plus the house by myself while working a full-time job? I mean, I know I'm fast and never sleep but..." He chuckled. "I have a few ranch hands. They have their own housing down by the road because sometimes I still don't trust myself to be around humans. Even though I have a few years under my belt, I still struggle with my *'sobriety'*. Sometimes when I'm really busy I forget to feed and I don't want to kill anyone by accident, especially when it could've easily been prevented. Just because we're vampires, it doesn't mean that we have to be monsters," he explained.

"I wholeheartedly agree, which is why I have to ask... Can I move in here with you until I can control myself? Once I get a job and can afford it, I'll get a place of my own. This way we'd also have more time to train." Kyra felt ashamed for asking, but she had nowhere safe to go.

"I was planning on *making* you stay, but I'd prefer that you were here willingly."

"*Make* me? Let's get one thing straight, *no one* can *make* me do anything I don't want to do. Also, if you try to hurt me in any way, I *will* kill you. Even if we're best friends, I will still hurt you if you hurt me. I'm so sick of people trying to put me in a box. The only thing I want is to experience true freedom. Is that too much to ask for?" They sat there in deafening silence while Kyra collected herself. "Can I sit here for a little bit longer?" Kyra was beginning to feel mentally exhausted already.

"Only if I can sit here with you. I've been so busy lately that I haven't had a moment to relax." He got quiet and they went back to sitting in silence. Kyra was thinking about the argument she had with her mom. The argument that led to where she is now. If she was being honest with herself, she didn't feel bad at all for what went down. Her mom had no right to criticize her when she kept the extent of her illness from her. As long as they were under the same roof, there would be constant fighting.

Kyra was beginning to feel like she was going to jump out of her skin, like she was on the edge of a windy cliff. Her mom had a way of getting under her skin, even if she wasn't anywhere near her.

She reached into her pocket to grab her phone so she could listen to music, but came up empty. Then she remembered that Jack still had her phone.

"Hey, Jack? Can I have my phone back please? I need it, like now," she asked as she tried to calm herself, trying not to let her panic show.

"I don't think so! Not until I can trust that you won't tell anyone our secret," he stated.

"Dammit, Jack! I only wanted to listen to my music! It helps keep me calm. Now give it to me, or I swear to god I'll *rip* your throat out!" Kyra was beginning to shake like she were having a panic attack.

Not good!

Jack reached into his back pocket and grabbed her phone, handing it to her. Kyra unlocked it frantically. She turned on her music and closed her eyes, taking slow, deep breaths. Novo Amor always helped her mid- panic attack while she was human. It was nice to see that that was still true.

After a couple of songs, Kyra was almost completely relaxed again. She opened her eyes and looked over at Jack. He looked slightly scared of her. *Good, serves him right.* Now he understood how she's been feeling while she kept her emotions in check.

She looked back out at the valley and that's when it hit her. The reason why she couldn't find the right words to describe the sunrise, it was because it was more of a feeling. When she saw the sunrise, she got the same feeling she did whenever she listened to Novo Amor. Maybe the singer, Ali John Meredith-Lacey, was also a vampire? It would be really cool if he were, because Kyra had been wanting to meet him for quite some time now. She thought it would be nice to see what had inspired his music.

"Have you turned anyone else, or is it just me?" Kyra asked. That was a question that she had been dying to ask.

"No, it's just you. This life isn't something I'd wish on anyone. Yes, there are a ton of perks, but it gets really boring. Once you've done everything there is to possibly do in the world, what's left?" Kyra felt like he was lying to her.

"Then why did you bother turning me? I doubt it's that boring. You just need to find a way to enjoy the simple things again," she said while shrugging her shoulder.

"Really? Like what? What kind of simple things could I possibly enjoy? Hmm?" Jack was clearly becoming annoyed with her.

"Maybe the fact that you're still *alive*? Whomever attacked you could've *easily* killed you, yet here you are. So maybe you should look at it like you've been given a second chance at life. Now you have all the time in the world to make a difference. Don't you want to make a positive impact on the world? I know I do." Kyra hoped she could get through to him because she couldn't imagine going through eternity without him there by her side to help guide her.

"I never thought of it like that... But what could I possibly do that would make any difference? Even though I have special abilities, I'm still just one person." Jack still didn't seem convinced.

"Seriously, Jack? You're a paramedic! You save lives every single day! That right there makes a big difference. You could also volunteer in a soup kitchen, or tutor children. Like I said, there are *plenty* of things you can do. When you help others without expecting anything in return, *that's* when you make a difference. One grain of rice can tip the scale. Meaning that each person has the ability to change the world. But it's still up to you to decide what kind of impact you want to make. So, what do you want to do?"

They sat there in silence while Jack mulled everything over. Kyra could tell that he was thinking really hard, which meant he actually *did* want to live. His coldness was just a facade- a mask to prevent her from seeing his true feelings.

"What if we created a huge garden on the property and used the food to help feed the homeless? Just because they're less fortunate doesn't mean that they don't deserve fresh, healthy food too. Or, if we can create a big enough garden, maybe we could donate some of the food to local schools? I remember how tiny and crappy the lunches were in school. It seemed like every day I was still so hungry that it felt as if I hadn't eaten anything at all. No child should ever have to feel hunger. So... what do you think?"

It was as if he had taken the thoughts right out of her mind. That had been a dream of hers for as long as she could remember. It was almost word for word from her own thoughts. Kinda creepy, but maybe they were just that good of a match that they shared a lot of the same interests.

"That's a great idea, Jack," she said, a huge grin spreading across her face. "When would you like to get started? If we start now it will have to be an indoor garden, and we'll need UV lights. If we tried planting anything outside at this time of year it'll just freeze and die. We'll need heaters too."

"I was thinking the same thing. Maybe we could use the barn? I know it probably doesn't hold the best of memories for you, but I'd like to change that. Would that be okay with you?" Jack looked a little worried, like he was waiting for her to lash out at him- or like she was about to catch him in a lie.

"That would be perfect, Jack," she smiled. "That would make it so much easier since there's already electricity running out to the barn. Plus, we'd have enough room to either grow a lot of one thing, or a variety of things. Could we start right away? When there's something I'm excited about, my patience is non-existent..." She didn't know of anywhere nearby where they could buy some UV lamps, so she'd have to look online. Maybe *Amazon* would have some?

Kyra could feel herself becoming manic, so she closed her eyes and took several slow, deep breaths to calm down. Now that she could organize her thoughts again, what they needed to do was some research and figure out what they wanted to grow and how much space each plant would need. Then they needed to figure out what kind of soil they'd need to buy, because they could have all the UV lamps in the world, but it wouldn't do them any good if the soil they used wasn't fertile. They had a lot of planning to do before they could plant anything, so Kyra figured it would be at least a week before they got to the planting part.

"Before we start though, I think we should do some research and draw up a layout of where everything is going to go. It will make things go a lot faster in my opinion. What do you think, Jack? Are you ready for this?" She asked, barely able to contain her excitement.

"I'm ready if you are, but I'm starting to think that maybe we should do your training first... We'll obviously need to make some supply runs and we can't have you slaughtering the whole town and outing our kind. We could test you out on one of the ranch hands first, but... I'll have to chain you to the chair again..." He looked like he wanted to kick himself just for mentioning the chair.

"That's okay, Jack. How long will the ranch hand have to be in the room with me?..." She asked nervously. She was so scared of just hurting someone, let alone possibly killing them.

"For however long it takes for you to stay in control. We have all the time in the world, so don't worry if you don't get it the first time around," Jack told her as he got up from the porch swing. They were now face to face and Kyra found herself staring up at him. She knew she was starting to develop feelings for him, but she did her best to push those unwanted feelings far from her mind. There was no time for those kinds of distractions right now and the memories of the car crash were still too fresh in her mind for her to be able to ignore them for the possibility of some silly crush she might be developing.

"So, does this ranch hand know what he's in for?..." She asked warily.

"No, but I'm going to compel him to forget once we're done anyway." He looked so proud of himself, but Kyra knew he was forgetting a *big* part.

"Um... Don't you think you're forgetting something? You know, something *important?*" She asked him. His brow furrowed as he thought about it.

"Nope. Not that I can think of," he replied, shrugging his shoulders.

"What if I *kill* him?! What then, huh? I'm pretty damn sure that it's impossible to compel a dead person! There are people that would miss him- people that would know he was missing." Kyra couldn't help but panic. This was the first big step in her new life. Was she really up for this kind of life? Not that she actually had any choice in the matter now since the choice had been taken away from her.

"Kyra, Kyra. *Kyra!* Listen! Everything will be okay! You need to have some faith in yourself. Believe that you can do it and you'll see that you had nothing to worry about." He pulled her into a hug, rubbing her back as he said, "I believe in you, Kyra. Remember that."

"I hope you're right, Jack..." She pulled away from him and

walked back into the house, leaving him standing there alone on the porch. She walked into the kitchen to put her teacup in the sink and get a glass of water, then went to her room to get her notebooks. With her stuff in hand, Kyra went to sit in the living room next to the fireplace. There was so much natural light in the house, but the light and warmth from the fire drew her in.

Kyra sat there for several minutes just listening to the crackling and popping of the logs in the fireplace. Her brain felt like it was going a million miles an hour and she was having trouble sorting through her thoughts.

With all of her inner turmoil, Kyra decided to start writing in all down. She had never been the type of girl to have a diary, but now would be a good time to start. She'd think of it as a way of documenting the start of her long existence.

Tuesday, October 29th, 2019
7:45am

I've never had a diary or a journal before, so here goes nothing... Over the past month, my life has been turned completely upside down. It started with an incident at work with my supervisor who is a bitch and a racist. Then, only a few short days ago, I became a vampire...

I know, sounds crazy, right? Last week, if someone told me that vampires were real, I would've thought they were crazy and had them locked up in a mental institution. I mean, this can't be real... can it? Does that also mean that other supernatural creatures exist?

I figured that if I wrote everything down that it would help me make sense of all this craziness. But where do I even start?... Do I start from the beginning, or do I deal with what's right in front of me? You know what? I'm going to make a list of my priorities and check them off as I go.

Priorities:
1) Move out of parent's house and move in with Jack.
2) Control thirst/hunger around humans.
3) Train/hone new vampire abilities.
4) Come up with gardening plans.
Okay, now that I can actually see in front of me, I definitely need to control my thirst **first** and foremost. Everything else is small potatoes in comparison.

Even though I'm scared about the possibility of hurting the ranch hand- or anyone else for that matter- I need to believe in myself. I just need to constantly remind myself of all my accomplishments so far, no matter how small they may seem in comparison.

"Hey, Kyra. It's time. Meet me down at the barn in a few minutes," Jack said from the doorway, startling her.

"Okay, I'll be right there," she replied, looking back down at her journal.

Time to go now. I'm meeting Jack in the barn so he can chain me to the chair before the ranch hand shows up. Hopefully this won't be my last- and only- entry... I'll be strong, I promise.

A few minutes later, after going to the bathroom, Kyra was in the doorway of the barn. She didn't want to do this, but it was necessary and she couldn't put it off forever. Taking a deep breath, Kyra stepped into the barn.

"Are you ready?" Jack asked. She nodded and sat on the chair. Kyra flinched when the cold chains touched her bare skin. "Sorry, did I hurt you?" He asked.

"No, the chains are cold. Keep going. I just want to get this done and over with." Her palms were clammy and her breathing was quick and shallow. Her stomach felt like a pit of acid from her anxiety.

Once he was done tightening the chains, Jack left the barn.

It felt like hours had gone by, but Kyra knew it couldn't have been more than fifteen minutes. Then she heard the sound of crunching gravel...

CHAPTER ELEVEN

The first thing she heard was the gravel under their boots as they approached. As they got closer, Kyra could hear the ranch hand's heartbeat and the ticking from his watch- which was nearly in sink with his heartbeat. It was deafening in the otherwise silence. She was busy focusing on her breathing when the barn door opened and they walked in...

He didn't look scared at all. He looked dazed, as if he wasn't there mentally. His heartbeat remained steady and he showed no sign of fear. She eyed them warily as Jack led him to a chair across from Kyra, then went to stand by the door. Kyra had been holding her breath since before the door had opened, but she couldn't hold it in any longer. She let out a long, shaky breath and breathed in.

Kyra didn't know what she was expecting, but nothing happened. She could still hear his steady heartbeat, and she could feel the warmth from his body, but it wasn't bothering her at all. There was no difference between this man and Jack when it came to tempting my thirst.

"Jack, I feel fine… Like, seriously, I don't feel anything. Was I supposed to be crazed with hunger or something?"

His forehead scrunched in confusion.

"Okay… Let's try something else then." He took something out of his pocket and walked back over to the ranch hand. The ranch hand gasped, but Kyra didn't have to see to know what happened. She could smell the blood instantly and she became queasy and light headed as she tried to hold her breath again. She could remember the taste of blood and how amazing it was, but the smell was so overpowering that she lost control of her stomach.

Turning her head to the side, Kyra threw up and couldn't stop. As long as she could still smell the blood, she wasn't sure if she could stop. Maybe once her stomach was completely empty? She sure was doing a crappy job at the whole vampire thing.

"Get him… out of here!" Kyra yelled at Jack in between throwing up.

"Why? Are you going to kill him?" He asked, but didn't do anything to help her out.

"No! The smell is revolting! Please, just get him out of here! Or let me go so I can get some air. Jack, please!" She pleaded with him. He nodded and reached down to help the completely unfazed ranch hand out of the chair.

They couldn't get out of the barn fast enough for Kyra and she threw up again. If Kyra were still human, that would be the moment she would have fainted.

"Are you okay now?" Jack asked as he walked back into the barn. The scent had left with the ranch hand and Kyra's stomach began to ease.

"Yeah, I'm good now. So, did I pass?…"

"To be honest… I'm not entirely sure. I've never heard of a vampire reacting like that to the smell of blood. Something about you is really off… Not in a bad way, I just mean that I'm not sure anymore if you're actually a vampire… It's like your humanity is rejecting vampirism, or maybe you weren't even human to begin with." He sat down in the other chair and stared at her intently.

"Well, I don't know if there's any truth to it, but I've heard my parents talking and they said that my grandmother is the reason why we moved here. Supposedly, she's Pagan and practices old witchcraft- but I'm sure I just heard them wrong." She could still remember sneaking past her parent's room at night and hearing bits and pieces of their arguments. Maybe they were just upset with her grandmother's choice in religion and didn't want her to influence their children? Who knows, maybe she just imagined the whole thing.

"Do you have her number? You could call and ask her. Wait, have you even met her before?" He asked. That was one of the first personal questions he had asked her so far, which struck her as a little odd since he seemed to already know everything about her.

"I've met her only a few times and I always thought she was a little eccentric. She was really nice though. She even sends me presents for my birthday. I might have her number in my phone but I'm not sure. We'll have to call soon though because she's eight hours ahead of us, but um… Hey, Jack? You kind of need to, you know, unchain me first…" She chuckled nervously, motioning with her head to the chains still wrapped around her torso.

"Shit! Sorry!" He seemed flustered for some reason. "So, are you going to talk to your grandma alone, or do you need me to be with you?" He asked as he undid the chains.

"Well, I was hoping you'd be there with me in case she has any questions that I don't know how to answer."

"Alright, let's get started," he said, handing her phone back to her hesitantly.

"Could we do it in the house? I never want to sit in this chair ever again. Especially when there's vomit all over the floor..." She grimaced.

"Sure. Let's go," he said. They walked back up to the house in silence, but all Kyra could think about was how *badly* she needed to brush her teeth. She was embarrassed about having thrown up in front of Jack, but there was nothing she could've done differently.

A small part of Kyra's brain noticed how close Jack was to her as they walked. She could've easily reached out and grabbed his hand, but they couldn't afford any distractions right now.

They reached the house and Kyra headed straight to the bathroom. She could hear Jack pause for a second before continuing to follow her. She walked into the bathroom and closed the door before Jack could come in.

"Are you going to throw up again?" He asked. Kyra could hear the anxiety in his voice and instantly felt bad.

"No, I'm okay. I just needed to brush my teeth and shower really quick to get rid of the vomit smell," she explained through the door.

"Okay, I'll be in the living room when you're ready."

Kyra heard him walk away and waited until he went to another part of the house before she started brushing her teeth. She took her time to brush her teeth, but showered at vamp speed. She was nervous about the phone call and wanted to get it over with. Kyra had always had anxiety when it came to talking to people on the phone, even if she had known them most of her life.

"Time to call your grandma now," Jack said as Kyra walked up behind him, now dressed in her comfiest pair of sweatpants and her baggy hoodie.

"Okay, okay," she sighed. "Let's get this over with." She took her phone from her pocket and clicked on her grandma's number. She took a deep breath and waited for it to start ringing. She wasn't looking forward to seeing next months' phone bill just from one international phone call.

"The number you have dialed can't come to the phone right now. Please leave your name, number, and a message after the beep." Kyra hung up and sighed.

"It went straight to voicemail. I could try calling again in an hour, but it'll be kinda late by then... Actually, I'll just wait and call again tomorrow."

"Why didn't you leave a message?" He asked, an edge of bitter irritation to his voice.

"She never checks her voicemail, so there's no point. I'll just call her again first thing in the morning. It's not like I have to worry about oversleeping anymore." She let out a nervous laugh and set her phone down on the glass coffee table.

"So, what now? Clearly, you can be around humans without wanting to rip their throats out. Does that mean you're ready to head back home? I know you don't want to see your mom, but you're gonna have to. Just tell her that you're moving out and you're only there to get the rest of your things. You don't even have to give her a reason why." He was very convincing, but that didn't do anything to help Kyra's nerves or the knot forming in her stomach. Surely her mother would notice the new changes to her appearance and would think she's even more of a mistake than she already does. Her mother would probably even go as far as trying to lock her up in some sort of institution.

"Could I, uh, eat first? I threw up all the blood from this morning." Kyra wasn't 'hungry' but she didn't want to be hangry while they were in town.

"Sure, no problem."

They walked into the kitchen where Jack got a blood bag from the fridge and poured some into a cup for her. Kyra could smell it from across the room so she took a deep breath and held it in. She drank it as fast as she could so she wouldn't have to taste it- it was bad enough having to smell it.

"Okay, I'll text my mum now and let her know that we'll be there in a little bit. If she's at work while we're there, then I'll leave a note with your address on it. Even though we're on bad terms right now, she still has the right to know where I am. Plus, I don't think you'd want the cops showing up at your house looking for me. She's controlling enough to report me as missing and then play the part of the loving mother to try and get sympathies from strangers."

"Do you know if anyone else will be home?" He asked with a worried look on his face, like he was afraid to meet her family. She didn't blame him, her family was a bit of a disaster.

"They shouldn't be. My dad should be away for work, and Bryton and Chloe are at school, so it might be just my mum." Kyra grabbed her phone and texted her mom as she talked to Jack. "Okay, are you ready to go? I want to get this over with as soon as possible."

"Yeah, come on. The truck is over in the shop, so we don't

have to walk clear down to the barn again. How much stuff do you need to pack?" He asked, hesitating before grabbing the keys.

"I don't know, maybe four boxes worth? I don't have very many clothes or shoes. Mostly what needs to be packed are my books and movies. I sold a lot of my stuff over the summer because I was planning on redoing my room and I needed the money for it. The furniture will have to stay since my parents paid for all of it."

Thankfully she didn't have very many belongings because that meant they could get in and out of the house really fast, possibly even faster if they used their vamp speed.

Kyra went to the bathroom because she didn't want to have to go again while they were at her parent's house so they could make a quick getaway. If she needed to pee again at some point on their way back, they could always stop somewhere along the way and maybe even get some lunch once they were done since it would be around lunch time by the time they got back to the house.

By the time they left, it was a few minutes after ten in the morning and Kyra was a bundle of nerves.

CHAPTER TWELVE

Jack was quiet the whole way into town. Kyra didn't really care because she was too preoccupied with looking out the windows at the new world flying past her. It still felt so surreal...

Unfortunately, the beauty around her didn't do much to alleviate the feeling of dread in her gut. She knew she had no reason to be afraid of her mom, but she couldn't help but feel like she were a child again and about to get a butt whoopin'.

They got to her parents' house about thirty minutes later and thankfully there weren't any cars in the driveway when they pulled up. She fumbled with her keys as she got out of the car and dropped them because her hands were shaking so badly. Before she could bend down to pick them up, Jack had already picked them up and placed them back in her hand.

Why couldn't she catch them before they fell? Maybe it was just her nerves? Who knows. She just needed to get this done and over with before anyone came home. She couldn't handle the screaming match that was bound to happen.

Once inside, they rushed up the stairs to her room and closed the door, locking it behind them. Even though no one was home, she didn't want to take any chances just in case her mom came home for her lunch break.

Kyra had been preparing for this moment, so she had a stack of empty storage totes in the top of her closet. She had Jack pack up her books and movies while she folded her clothes and packed them as tightly as she could into one tote. Since Jack had a ton of hygiene products at his house, Kyra didn't bother grabbing her things from the bathroom. She grabbed her favorite pillows off her bed and put them in the tote with the movies to help keep them from moving around during transport. They unlocked her door and carried her stuff down the stairs.

After they loaded her things into Jack's car, Kyra jumped into the passenger seat and reclined it so that- to anyone passing by- it would look like Jack was the only person in the car. She didn't want to take any chances of someone seeing her and notice her sudden change in appearance. Some of them were friends with her parents. She also didn't want them to report back to her mother that they saw her with a guy that wasn't her best friend- her best friend that she was supposed to be staying with.

"Hey, Jack. Could we stop at the store and get some ice cream?" Ice cream had always helped when she was having a bad day. Plus, it's not like she had to worry about getting fat anymore.

"You know it's *winter*, right?..." Jack asked, flabbergasted.

"So? I eat it all year long," she chuckled.

"Okay, whatever you say... Would you mind if I went ahead

and did my grocery shopping? There's no point in making another trip to town since we're already here," Jack pointed out.

"Sure, as long as we can get more cornbread mix too," Kyra laughed. Jack laughed along with her and Kyra felt her face go red. His laugh was one of the most beautiful sounds she had ever heard. It was a deep, but not too loud, throaty chuckle- she couldn't quite explain it. She wished she had kept quiet because now he was staring at her with an inquisitive look.

Shit…

He started the car and it took them only a few minutes to get to the store from her parent's house. Once they were parked, Kyra looked over to see that Jack was looking at her once again.

"We should probably go in the store now…" Kyra suggested, opening her car door. She didn't give him a chance to respond before she got out of the car and was halfway across the parking lot.

"Kyra! Hold up!" Jack yelled as he jogged over at a human pace. He grabbed her arm and stopped her. "Are you *trying* to get us caught?!" He looked furious and Kyra was so taken aback that she immediately began to tear up. His sudden shift in attitude made her completely forget any feelings she had just had about him.

"What are you talking about?" She asked barely above a whisper.

"Kyra, you just went at vamp speed in broad daylight…" His eyes were wide. He looked scared.

"I'm sorry…" She sniffled. "It'll be okay, Jack. I'm super short, remember. If anyone happened to see me, they would've assumed I was running, or they'd think that they just imagined it. Don't worry about it. If anything happens, you can just compel them to forget. Now, can we get our shopping done? Just carry on as if nothing happened." He nodded, but still had panic written in every feature of his face. Kyra knew he wasn't going to relax so she grabbed his hand and held it as they walked to the front of the store. Now he looked shocked and his cheeks were pink bright pink- which any onlooker would assume was from the crisp morning autumn air.

Once they got to the front of the store, Kyra let go of his hand and grabbed a cart. She needed the distraction and a reason to not hold his hand again. She had no idea what he needed to get, so she motioned for him to take the cart. Kyra was careful to keep her distance and she made sure to keep at least five feet of space between them at all times.

They made it to the ice cream aisle, but Jack seemed to already know what kind she wanted. Kyra inwardly rolled her eyes.

Of course, he did.

She liked cookie dough ice cream, but she always put either peanut butter or caramel sauce on top. It had been her favorite for as long as she could remember. When she was little, she liked to make weird food concoctions- most of which were disgusting- but that one had been her crowning masterpiece.

The whole time they were shopping, Kyra couldn't help but feel like she was being watched. Maybe it was her new appearance, but her gut was telling her that something wasn't right. There were people looking at her when she would walk by them and their faces would turn red when she'd make eye contact.

Was she really that attractive now? She had spent so much of her life trying to be invisible that the sudden attention was unnerving. It made her skin crawl and she was ready to get back to the house and hide under the bed.

Jack steered their cart to one of the checkout lanes, but the store was busy so it was going to be at least another fifteen minutes before they could get back in the car. Kyra was antsy and fidgeted with her bracelet while they stood in line. She could feel people giving her weird looks, but she couldn't do anything to stop the panic attack.

Jack let go of the cart and wrapped his arms around her. He rested his chin on her head and Kyra buried her face in his chest. The world around her quieted. With each deep breath, Kyra could smell his cologne. She found the smell of musk and cedar wood to be very intoxicating and relaxing at the same time.

Her panic attack started to go away within a few seconds and was over less than a minute later. Kyra tried to keep the hug going for as long as she could but someone near them cleared their throat loudly. She opened her eyes, glaring at them and they immediately looked away before switching to another check stand. Served them right for being rude.

"Kyra, check stand nine just opened. Hurry!" Jack whispered in her ear. She rushed ahead of him to claim their spot. There was no way she was going to spend more time in the store than she had to so it was difficult for her to maintain a human pace.

To her surprise, she actually felt really tired, almost as if she could sleep an entire day away. She had honestly been through *so much* in the past twenty-four hours that it was a wonder she was still standing on her own two feet.

They were on their way out to the car not even five minutes later. Now they had a half an hour drive ahead of them... Well, more like twenty minutes if there was no traffic or red lights.

Kyra sat there looking out the passenger window as Jack started the car and pulled out of the parking lot. She avoided eye contact at all cost. Honestly, she had no idea what to say to him...

How could she bring up the intensity of the hug without admitting how it had made her feel? She's supposed to be fighting against having feelings for him, but then he goes and does things like that to weaken her resolve. Would it really be all that bad of an idea for them to date?...

"Should we talk about what happened back there?" Jack asked without looking away from the road.

"Nope," she replied, still looking out the window.

They were both silent for a few minutes.

"Okay... We really should talk about it though, but it can wait until later." Jack looked over at Kyra and he could tell right away that something wasn't right. She looked ill, almost like she was going to throw up or pass out and her skin was turning an odd, ashy color. He looked back at the road and pushed down harder on the gas pedal to get them home faster.

Normally, he would pull over and give her a blood bag, but he was advised by a 'friend' to not keep that kind of stuff in the car in case he was ever pulled over. There was no reason for a paramedic to keep bags of blood in his personal vehicle. Except for theft, of course.

"Hey, are you okay? You look like you're going to faint or something." He looked over at her again and this time she was looking back.

"I'm just really tired, like I could sleep for a whole day. I feel completely drained, mentally, and physically. If I had a battery percentage above my head, it would probably show ten percent." She sighed, reclined her seat a little bit and closed her eyes.

"Kyra, hey! Stay awake, okay! Just five more minutes!" Jack

pleaded, stepping on the gas even more. Kyra was looking more and more like death with each passing second. It was then that he realized she was starting to desiccate and she'd die if she didn't feed soon, *very* soon. He felt so stupid for not having any blood in the car. He should have known better that a new vampire wouldn't be able to go as long without blood as he could.

He slowed down enough to make the turn into his driveway, then floored it again. He stopped mere inches from hitting the garage door and leaped out of the car, running at vamp speed to the house and grabbed several blood bags from the fridge before running back to the car.

He had only been gone for a few short seconds, but it felt like a lifetime to Kyra. Jack flung her door open and unlatched her seat belt. She was so gray by this point that he feared he was too late. He propped her head up- as her chin had been touching her chest- opened her mouth and poured some blood in, hoping that he wasn't too late. He had no purpose in life if she didn't make it through this. She was his whole world...

Kyra coughed, gasping for air, and looked up at Jack. He had a grin spreading across his face with a couple tears sliding down his cheeks. She didn't acknowledge him, except for yanking the blood bags from his hands. She completely drained the first two bags, and didn't start to feel okay until she was finishing up the third one.

Closing her eyes, she took a slow, deep breath, letting the warmth spread through her body again. The anxiety that she had been feeling only shortly before was gone and she relaxed.

"What the *hell* just happened?!" She asked, not able to wrap her mind around it as she reclined back onto the seat.

"I'm not sure... It was like your body thought it had been

weeks since you had blood instead of only a couple of hours. How're you feeling now? Are you still tired at all?" He asked.

"I feel fine, like nothing ever happened... Maybe I just have a fast metabolism or something," she suggested. It was a very logical reasoning, but her gut was telling her otherwise.

"Let's get you inside. Why don't you lay down on the couch for a bit while I make us some lunch? Then, after we eat, we can try to figure out what's been going on with you." Jack helped her inside to the couch, then went back outside to get the groceries and to bring in her totes of stuff from the car to the mudroom.

To be honest, Kyra felt fine, completely fine as if nothing had happened. What the hell was going on with her? It's like her body was trying to reject being a vampire. Who knows anymore- maybe she really wasn't human to begin with.

Jack brought in some chips and sandwiches, then went back for their sodas. Kyra wasn't hungry for human food but she didn't want to be rude so she ate it anyway. Maybe part of the problem was that she needed to maintain an equal diet of both blood and human food in order for her body to even be able to process the blood.

Neither of them spoke or even looked at the other while they ate. Jack was afraid to look at her because he didn't want to see it if she began to desiccate again- he couldn't bare it another time. His heart had gone through so much in the past twenty-four hours that, if he were human, he probably would've been having a heart attack right now.

He had loved Kyra since the first time he saw her back in high school. He had spent months watching her from a distance before he had worked up the courage to talk to her. Jack was so nervous that he forgot what he was going to say and ended up asking if she had a pencil he could borrow.

He felt like a moron back then, but now he's getting the chance to start over. But who knew how long he'd have with her... If she were to die to tomorrow, he honestly didn't know how he'd be able to cope with the loss. He'd probably go on a murderous rampage and become a serial killer or something...

Ding-dong.

Jack and Kyra looked at each other when the doorbell rang. Who would come all the way out here? Was it the cops? Had someone reported Jack for speeding? Was it Kyra's mom coming to cause trouble? They set their sandwiches down and walked over to the front door. Jack opened the door to see a stranger standing there.

"Can I help you ma'am?" He asked. She ignored him.

"Hello, sweetheart," she replied, looking around him to Kyra.

"*Grandma?!*" Kyra gasped.

CHAPTER THIRTEEN

"*Grandma*?! What are you doing here? How did you find me?" Kyra asked in astonishment.

"You're my granddaughter- my blood. I felt your distress and took the first flight out I could get. I'm here to help."

Kyra stood there staring at her grandmother, not knowing what to say. Her mind was reeling from the shock of seeing her grandma in front of her- literally the last person she would've imagined to be at the door. Jack didn't have the same problem, but he definitely seemed almost equally as surprised as she was.

"Would you like to come in, ma'am? You've come a very long way to see Kyra, you can come inside and rest if you like. We just sat down for lunch, I would be more than happy to make you something as well." Jack was being a total gentleman to Kyra's grandmother and it warmed her heart. Her grandmother clearly didn't feel the same way as she glared at him, eyeing him warily. Her behavior reminded Kyra of either a cat arching its back and hissing, or a dog with its hackles up and emitting a low growl. Either way, she was *not* comfortable around Jack, which upset Kyra.

"I'd prefer to stay right here, thank you very much. May I please speak to my granddaughter? *Alone.*" Kyra could tell that her grandmother was trying to be civil, but the *hostility*? Why was *she* mad at Jack when he was being nothing but polite?

"No problem. I'll be in the office if you need me," he said, turning around and walking away- which left Kyra there facing her grandma alone. Kyra motioned to the porch swing and they walked over and sat down.

"Now will you answer me? How did you know where to find me? I tried calling you this morning, but you didn't answer. So how did you know when I was in trouble?" Kyra questioned.

"I've been watching over you since you were born. When you were born, I did a connection spell so I could always feel what you were feeling physically and emotionally. Then, suddenly, the other day I could barely feel your presence anymore. It was like your life force was hanging on by a thread." Her grandmother looked beyond worried- like Kyra could drop dead at any moment. She still felt fine, but who knew how long it would last... There was no way she was about to tell her grandma about what happened less than an hour ago.

"A connection spell? As in magic? Real magic? Something bad is happening to me, right? Gran, I'm scared..." Kyra's eyes welled with tears.

Her grandmother grasped her hands in her own. Kyra felt like there were suddenly no more secrets between them, like her grandma already knew everything she was wanting to tell her about the past few days.

"I know, my sweet granddaughter, I know you are," she replied.

"Do you know what's happening to me? *Please*, tell me you know how to help. Please, gran." Kyra began to cry and her grandma pulled her into a hug. The fabric of her grandma's sweater was soft like a cloud and had a light smell of herbs and earth. Normally, the smell of her grandmother's home would bring her complete comfort, but today was not one of those days, as Kyra was now facing the most difficult day of her life.

"I do, but you're not going to like what I have to say. You're dying sweetie… You weren't human to begin with and now your body is rejecting life itself. You were a witch, Kyra. Jackson had no right to do what he did to you." Kyra sat up so fast that she nearly knocked her poor grandmother off the porch swing.

"I was a *witch*?! Why didn't you ever tell me?! Do you realize how much that would have helped me? I could've been happy, totally happy this entire time! I could've cured my illness years ago and felt like a normal human being, instead of feeling like a complete nut job."

"I was only following your mother's wishes. The magic skips a generation and she was jealous when she found out you were a witch. She had me do a suppression spell so your powers wouldn't manifest in order to keep you safe. After trying for years to get pregnant, your mother came to me for help. I called upon Freya to help your mother. She didn't have to help her, but Freya clearly had big plans for you. Kyra, you are a daughter of Freya- your powers come directly from the goddess of love, fertility, and beauty. She won't take too kindly to you throwing those powers away," her grandmother stated.

"You mean the powers I didn't even know existed until a few

seconds ago? I'm sure she'll understand- she *is* a Goddess after all. Maybe she already knew this was going to happen. Maybe this is what she was planning for me to become," Kyra pondered. "So, if you undid the spell, would that fix everything? Would I be able to become a vampire, or would I die instantly?" Kyra asked.

"Removing the spell won't kill you, but in order for you to live, you have to make a choice. Either completely reject becoming a vampire and stay a witch, or sacrifice an innocent human and stay a vampire forever. As a witch, that makes you a protector of nature and the karmic scales, meaning that you can never take a life. Whichever you choose, you can't be both- you can *never* be both. As a vampire, you *will* have special abilities since you weren't human to begin with, but will that be worth sacrificing an innocent human?" Her grandmother stared at her as if it was the easiest decision in the world. Her decision wouldn't just change *her* life, but so many others as well. There *had* to be some other way...

"What if I fed on someone that was already dying? Would that work?" Kyra asked. Her grandma shook her head.

"No, their life force has already been claimed. You'll have to feed on someone that is full of life and completely drain them," her grandmother replied.

"What about a murderer? Would that work? I'd be getting a killer off the streets and the world would be better off without them. I would only have to take one life and that could save a least one other life, which would help keep the scales balanced."

Kyra found herself crossing her fingers. She didn't want to die, but she already knew deep down in her gut that she didn't want to be a witch. How could she be a witch when the person she loved was a vampire?

"Yes…" Her grandmother hesitated. "It's possible, but it's extremely dangerous because of how unpredictable it can be. It'll only work if their 'body count' is high enough. When they kill someone, part of the victim's soul attaches to theirs. The only way to make absolute certain, they will have had to have *at least* three victims. Their 'life force' should be strong enough to complete your transition.

"Kyra… You only have a few more days to live either way- no matter which you decide. You have until the setting of the next full moon." Kyra's stomach sank and she felt like throwing up. How were they going to find the right killer in time? If law enforcement could barely catch murderers in months- years even- then how could *they* find one within the next few days before she dies? Who knew how much longer her strength would last before she'd begin to desiccate again.

"How can we possibly find a murderer before I die? Is there *anything* you can do, gran? Please?… I know you hate the idea of me being a vampire, but I want to be one more than anything. I'll have an eternity to keep making the world a better place. I want to make a world where peace and happiness exist. Please, gran, please help me do this," Kyra pleaded with her grandmother.

"There is something I could do, but I don't know if it will work… Murder isn't natural and it darkens a person's soul. I could do a locator spell, but instead of looking for a person, I'd be looking for the darkness they harbor. I'll be focusing on the darkest energies so we can be certain that their sacrifice will be enough. There's no guarantee that it will even work, or that we'll be able to find them in time if it does. If it comes down to it, and you'd rather live, I could get the spell ready so you can stay a witch. At least that way you could live for a little longer than a natural human life."

Her grandmother looked so distraught that it broke Kyra's heart just looking at her. She knew she only wanted what was best for her, but all Kyra wanted was the ability to decide for herself when she was going to die. More than anything, she wanted to make the world a better place.

"Gran? Do you know if vampires can have children? I know the children wouldn't be human, but is it even possible?" Kyra wanted to have a child someday, but if that wasn't possible, she'd be okay with adopting instead. Becoming a vampire was still something she wanted, even if she couldn't have children of her own.

"I have no idea. I'm sorry my dear... If that's something you want, why don't you stay a witch? That way you'd be certain you could have children. Trust me, I'd love to have great-grandchildren, but it's all your decision."

"I still want to be a vampire, gran. There is so much *good* I could do but it all takes time, time I don't have. It would take even longer than a witch's life span to do everything I want to do. I could put an end to pollution and world hunger. Just imagine what life would look like! Gran, if you could see how I see everything, you'd know what I mean. Everything is so green right now, but it could be so much greener! The air would be so much cleaner too. Isn't that the kind of world you'd like to live in?" Kyra asked. She wished everyone in the world had the same dream as her, only because it would make it so much easier to save the planet.

"How do you plan on doing that? Do you even know the average lifespan of a witch? You're only one person. How much change could you bring about as one person?" Her grandma questioned.

"She's not alone, she has me," Jack said from the doorway, startling them both. "Would you like to come inside? I got a fire going and made some tea. I'm heading down to the barn to work so you'll have the house to yourselves." Jack walked across the porch and down the steps, walking over to the shop and got in his truck. Kyra looked over at her grandmother and saw her glaring after him.

"Look, gran. If you're going to be here, you need to give Jack a chance. He saved me when everyone else was busy trying to convince me that I was crazy. He saw me when no one else did. He gave me something I wanted, and he's been nothing but a total gentleman so far. He's even been nice to you when you've been hostile towards him from the second you got here. Gran, he's trying, okay? He *really* wants you to like him. Your opinions matter to him because they matter to me. Gran... He loves me, and if I'm being honest, I love him too. I want to have a long future with him. He's my soul mate. Don't ask how I know because I can't describe it- it's just a feeling I have." Kyra sighed and looked away. She couldn't believe she just said that out loud.

"Oh, Kyra. He's not good for you- he's a parasite! He'll be the death of you, one way or another. He's gotten you completely brainwashed. Why can't you see that? He's keeping you from your true potential." Her grandmother was furious- but so was she.

"Gran! He saved me *weeks* before I turned! I blacked out and hit my head on the pavement. *He* was the paramedic that showed up. *He* stayed at the hospital until he knew I was okay. *He's* the one who showed me that my mum wasn't who I thought she was. Did you know I had a brain tumor and she knew, but told the doctor not to tell me? Then continued to treat me like I was crazy? She's my mum- she's supposed to protect me, not keep secrets from me. I can't trust my own mother, so, yes, of course I'm giving Jack a chance. It's not as if I'm making it easy on him. He has to prove I can trust him before I give him a chance."

Kyra was angry and could feel herself becoming more upset. How could her grandmother think she was being stupid about the whole thing? She wasn't a kid anymore!

"I don't think you've thought any of this through. You're jumping in head first without thinking about the consequences. You don't even know him, Kyra! He's killed people before; I could feel it before he had opened the door. Kyra, he's pure evil! I wish you could see that. If I were to perform the spell, I know he would be on the map and probably the worst of them all."

"That's because he had no one to help him! He had no idea what was happening to him. He had to figure it out for himself. He was *alone*..." Kyra sighed and closed her eyes, getting control of her emotions. "Gran, he was barely even seventeen when he was attacked and turned against his will. I never expected him to be perfect. Has he made mistakes? Yes. Will he continue to make mistakes? Probably. That doesn't necessarily make him a bad person, so please quit treating him like one." Kyra was trying to be nice to her grandmother since she was one of the only people on her side as she was growing up, but at least now she knew where her mom got her denseness from.

"I'm going to go. I'll be back later with the ingredients for the spells. I hope you'll make the right choice..." With that said, Kyra's grandma got up off the porch swing and got into the waiting taxi. Kyra sat there, watching the taxi drive down the hill until she could no longer see it.

Instead of sitting around and moping about it, Kyra walked down to the barn to find Jack. They needed to prepare for tonight, but Kyra also wanted to spend as much time with Jack as possible, just in case tonight was an utter failure. This could end up being the last time they ever see each other.

Jack looked up as Kyra walked around to the front of the barn, then went back to sweeping the floor. Kyra grabbed another broom and they both swept in silence. They didn't look at each other and neither tried to start up the conversation. Kyra felt like Jack was upset with her, like maybe it was her fault that she was dying.

"Look, Jack. I'm not sure how much of our conversation you heard, but it's not my fault that I'm dying. I wasn't human to begin with."

"I know, I heard. I'm not mad at you, I'm just worried that we'll be too late to save you. If I had known that witches were real- and that you were one- then I would've waited to turn you and had a backup plan already in place," he explained. They were silent for a while as they finished sweeping out the barn.

"We need to stay positive that things will turn out for the better. If it comes down to the wire, then my grandmother can reverse my transition and I can go back to being a witch. At least that way I'll still be alive and maybe we could try again as soon as we found the right person I need to complete the transition."

Jack was quiet as he mulled that over. They kept sweeping as he thought carefully.

"But how can we be sure that you'd even get a second chance? What if you went back to being a witch but could never become a vampire again? It's not like we have a rule book for any of this."

Jack got quiet again and walked off, heading back to the house. Was she expected to follow him or something?… Kyra slowly began to follow after him once he was about halfway to the house.

When Kyra walked in the front door, Jack was nowhere to be seen. She closed her eyes and listened for the slightest sound of movement. After a few moments, she could hear a clicking sound, like someone typing on a keyboard. Kyra didn't want to bother him, so she figured she'd clean the bathroom to pass the time. Her mess was still there from this morning when she took a bath. Her clothes were so disgusting that she threw them in the garbage- even though she felt like setting them on fire would be a better solution because of the horrible smell that was coming from them.

Since there wasn't much else to do after cleaning the bathroom, Kyra got her phone out and opened *Google*. She was going to try and do a little bit of research on her own. Kyra had already been a fan of the supernatural, but that was before she knew it was real. Who really knew what other creatures were out there just out of sight? Clearly witches and vampires were real, but what about mermaids? Werewolves? Banshees? How did witches and vampires come into being? Were they both humans that had evolved into something greater as time passed? Or did someone or something create them?

Those were the biggest questions that might still be a complete mystery to humans and mystical creatures alike and they will more than likely stay that way for the rest of eternity.

CHAPTER FOURTEEN

Kyra startled when Jack came into her room. He set a glass of blood next to her on the nightstand. She had been so preoccupied that she hadn't noticed her thirst. Kyra looked out the window next to her bed and realized that it was dark outside. Hours had passed, but, to her, it felt like merely a few minutes had gone by. Her small notepad was nearly full of notes about both witches and vampires. But, even with all that research, nothing had come close to what she now knew to be true.

"You should drink this before your grandmother gets here. I'm pretty sure she won't take too kindly to you drinking it in front of her," Jack suggested.

"What were you working on in the office?" Kyra asked.

"I was looking for a way to help you. I couldn't stand around doing chores when I thought there might be a way to help you," he explained. Kyra got the feeling that that wasn't the whole story. She felt the urge to run but didn't know why. Her curiosity won over the urge, but she held the feeling in her mind because maybe there was something her body was trying to tell her.

"Then why did you walk off without saying anything? We could've worked together instead of doing the same research twice," she pondered.

"I couldn't look you in the eye, knowing that I might end up killing you. If I had just left you alone, you would still be human and *alive*. If you die, it will all be my fault. I was selfish because you were what I wanted most in this world, but I wasn't patient enough to fully think things through. I'm a horrible person that shouldn't be allowed to live if you die…"

"Jack! You are *not* a horrible person!" Kyra told him as she got up off the bed. "Could you have waited a little while longer? Probably. Could you have done something else rather than run me off the road? Most definitely. But you also saved my life. I don't take that kind of thing lightly and I thank you for that. If you hadn't turned me, I'd be at home right now laying in my bed, staring up at the ceiling, wishing I had a different life. I'd definitely be getting on my mom's nerves just by existing in my room while trying to stay out of her path."

"That doesn't make what I did any better, Kyra. I should've known better but I wasn't thinking clearly. I was thinking with the wrong head." He blushed at his lousy joke.

"It's okay, Jack! I'll prove it to you." Kyra pulled his head down to her level and kissed him. What happened next shocked Kyra to her very core.

As their lips touched, her mind was flooded with images of bloody corpses, burning bodies, and blood, blood, and more blood. But, with those images, also came sound and emotions.

Both his emotions and those of his victims. Kyra was seeing into the mind of a psychotic killer. She could still see and feel Jack, but she could also see herself through his eyes. Kyra gasped and pulled away- all their screams still echoing in her ears.

"You weren't supposed to see that..." He said with an evil look in his eyes. Kyra's blood turned to ice in her veins. How could she be so blind? Her own grandmother could feel it before she had even seen him, so how did she not see any of this coming? Kyra should've known something was wrong with him.

"You're going to kill me now, aren't you?" Kyra asked him shakily. Her heart was in her throat and her breath hitched in her chest as she struggled to clear her mind.

"Honestly? I'm not sure. When I told you I loved you, I meant it. What happens next is all up to you. You can either ignore what you just saw, or you can die. Choice is yours." Kyra didn't dare move a single muscle as he spoke for fear that he'd snap her neck if she so much as flinched. She felt like a deer in headlights and couldn't find the right words to say.

Just because she couldn't speak, that didn't mean her brain was mute as well. She was thinking back to what her grand-mother said earlier. She never said that the 'sacrifice' had to be human... And all of his victims had been innocent children- children who's bloody faces were now burned into the back of her eyelids.

"Can we pretend like none of this ever happened- including the kiss?" Kyra choked out. The memory of the kiss revolted her and she felt like there wasn't enough bleach in the world to rid herself of the feeling it left on her lips.

"Of course. Can I trust that you won't tell anyone about what you saw?" He asked, his eyes locked on hers, as if staring into her soul.

"Yes, totally!" She blurted out of fear.

Jack eyed her warily for a few moments before shrugging it off and smiling at her. Kyra grabbed her glass off the nightstand and slowly sipped the blood as a way to try and prove her point.

"Is there something you'd like for dinner? Your grandma should be here soon. Do you think she'd be okay to eat dinner with us?"

His mood shift only freaked her out even more. Only a true psychopath could change their attitude that quickly as if nothing happened.

"Sure, I don't see why not. Um, how about cheesy potato soup with chunks of bacon?" Kyra asked. "It's her favorite."

"Coming right up!" Jack declared, already in a chipper mood. He believed her so easily...

Kyra had finished the last of the blood in the glass as he was turning around to leave the bedroom. Kyra took that opportunity to smash the glass into the back of his head. Then her instincts took over and Kyra felt like her consciousness had left her body. She was aware of everything that was now happening, but more like she was watching a movie.

Stunned, Jack dropped to floor and, in his shocked state, Kyra had enough time to pick up a shard of glass and stab him in the neck repeatedly. Blood began to spray everywhere, but Kyra had her mouth to the wound, draining his blood before he could even have a chance to fight back. He tried to shake her off of his back, but was too weak. Less than a minute later, Jack was dead- every drop of blood drained from his body. Kyra collapsed onto the floor next to him and propped herself up against the foot of her bed.

It was only a few seconds later that Kyra realized something strange was happening to her. Her body kept getting warmer and warmer and her head felt like it might explode. She could hear the doorbell ring somewhere in the distance and she tried calling out for help.

Then, when she thought the pain couldn't get any worse, Kyra could feel the exact moment the magic left her body- like the snap of a rubber band. It felt as if she had been struck by Thor's hammer and she couldn't breathe.

Kyra collapsed to the floor next to Jack's body as she tried to step over him while trying to catch her breath. The doorbell rang again incessantly and Kyra dragged herself to the hallway before she had enough strength to get to her feet. In auto pilot mode, Kyra walked across the house to answer the door. In hindsight, she probably should've cleaned herself up first.

The moment she opened the door, her grandmother let out a blood- curdling scream. That scream was able to break Kyra free from the fogginess in her head. She looked down at herself and saw what had frightened her grandma. Kyra was *covered* in blood and it was even in her hair. She looked like she had just stepped off the set of *Carrie*. She started to hyperventilate as she realized what she'd done.

"Jack... He-he's dead... He's dead. Gran, what have I done?!" Kyra screamed, collapsing at her grandma's feet. She was completely hysterical, sobbing and wailing so loudly that her grandmother had to shout to be heard.

"Kyra... Kyra! Tell me what happened so I can help!" Kyra continued to wail. "I can't help if you don't tell me what happened. It's okay sweetheart, talk to me." Kyra's sobbing quieted as she went into shock.

"You were right," she whispered. "He wasn't who I thought he was... He tricked me. He was a murderer, just like you said.

How could I not see him- the real him? I'm such an idiot!"

"Oh, sweetie! It's not your fault. He knew your weaknesses and used them against you. That was how he was able to worm his way into your mind to control you. You can't blame yourself, sweetheart, your thoughts and actions were not your own. It was either you or him and you chose to live. You had to act in self-defense to save yourself. You are a *survivor*, Kyra. Now, can you stand up?" She helped Kyra to her feet and led her back inside the house.

"Where's Jack?" Her grandma asked.

"My bedroom floor, down the hallway, second door on the left," Kyra gasped as she tried to pull herself together.

"What about the bathroom? We need to get you cleaned up," she asked.

"It's across from my room. Gran? I can't see him, not like that… Can you go in there for me?" They were now in the hallway outside of her room.

"Of course, sweetie. How about you go get the shower started?"

"Okay…"

Her grandma went into her room and closed the door so Kyra wouldn't have to see anything. How were they going to explain this to the police? It's not like they could say she had been kidnapped since they had gone to the grocery store and plenty of people had gotten a good look at the two of them together.

Kyra couldn't focus on anything right now, let alone come up with a plan to get rid of Jack's body. *His body*…Kyra looked at herself in the mirror and couldn't move. She looked like she had just stepped out of a slasher movie. The blood had already begun to dry in her hair, turning it into a matted mess. Her green sweater was now brown and crusty looking, heavy with the weight of his blood.

Unfreezing from the spot in front of the mirror, Kyra went to turn on the shower. As it was warming up, she stripped off each piece of clothing carefully as to not make a bigger mess.

The second she stepped under the stream of water, it looked like Satan's falls. In order to protect her sanity, Kyra pretended that she was on her period and that was where the blood was coming from. It was hard to imagine, but she couldn't afford to go back into shock again. Not now.

She opened one bottle after another trying to cover up the rusty, metallic smell. She didn't even care if what she was using to wash her hair was actually body wash as long as it got the blood out of her hair.

It wasn't until Kyra had scrubbed every inch of her body multiple times that the water no longer ran red. She turned off the shower and grabbed a towel from the cubby shelf next to the shower. There was a fresh robe on the back of the door and she put it on while she dried her hair.

Knock, knock.

"Are you okay in there?" Her grandmother asked. Kyra opened the door.

"I'm not sure, gran. None of this seems real... Is he...is he really gone? Did I actually kill him?" Kyra's voice was so faint that her grandma had to lean in to hear her.

"Yes, sweetheart, I'm afraid so. Let me go grab you some clothes, then we can go from there, okay?"

"Okay." Her grandma closed the door again and Kyra went back to staring at herself in the mirror. She was actually really beautiful now, but her physical beauty was the complete opposite of what she felt on the inside. How could she ever like herself after what she'd just done? Granted, it wasn't like he was a great person, but that doesn't justify what she did. Now she was no better than he was.

"Here's your clothes. I wasn't sure what you wanted to wear so I just grabbed you something comfy. I'll go make us a fresh pot of tea while you get dressed."

Kyra was so lost in her thoughts that she hadn't heard her grandma knock on the door again before opening it.

"Thanks, grandma." Kyra dressed quickly, but froze as she stepped into the hallway. Even though her bedroom door was closed, she could still smell the blood, along with something else she couldn't place. Kyra continued down the hallway and met her grandma in the kitchen.

She was going to have to face the consequences of her actions, but she knew it would break her if she went into her room right now. Maybe once they had a plan, then she could start to feel at peace with what she did. She had promised herself that she wouldn't have a body count, but Jack forced her hand. The images from Jack's mind were now seared into hers and it terrified her. How many innocent people had he killed? How many families were waiting for their loved ones to come home? How many families had been torn apart by that psychopath?

"Why don't we go sit by the warm fire while we have our tea?" Her grandma suggested. Kyra nodded and followed her into the living room. The warmth from the tea and the fire spread through Kyra's body and it wasn't until then that she realized how cold she really was. The shock was wearing off as she warmed up.

"How're you feeling?" Her grandma asked.

"A little better. I feel really odd though, like my emotions are muted. It feels off, like I'm not me. I don't know how to explain it exactly," she explained.

"That's because you're finishing your transition. It should be over soon. Once it's done, you might feel like you're on an emotional roller coaster because you'll start feeling what your mind and body are currently trying to put off. We should take advantage of that numbness while it lasts though. We should come up with a plan to take care of Jack."

"Are we going to call the police?" Kyra asked. She wasn't scared to go to prison, but someone would surely notice when she wasn't aging like everyone else.

"Oh, hell no. There's no way to explain this without exposing our world. There's a reason why the supernatural are still considered to be myths."

"Well, we can't just bury him and pretend like nothing happened because someone would more than likely come looking for him," Kyra pointed out.

"You could file a missing person's report in a few days and say that your *friend* went to the coast for a day trip and hasn't come back and that his phone keeps going to voicemail." Her grandma was definitely a little obsessed with stereotypical crime shows.

"There are ways to track a cell phone and it would show that he never left the house. Then they would come here and search the property. Boom, caught." Kyra watched too many crime shows to not think of every possibility. They sat in silence as they tried to think of anything even remotely possible that wouldn't end with Kyra going to prison.

"How about we go through the paperwork in his office or try to find a safe. He admitted to me that he had been following me for a while, which means he's bound to have notes or other kinds of documents about me. We could burn anything mentioning me, then build up the fire in the fireplace to where it could easily start a house fire. No one else besides mum even knows I'm here, so we could just walk away," Kyra explained.

"What about those guys that were working in the field when I pulled up earlier today?" Her grandma asked.

"They're fine. Only one of them has seen me, but Jack compelled him to forget about me. The others were told to stay away from the house and the upper barn." Kyra could see the pieces finally coming together. Now it made sense why she wasn't allowed to react with any of Jack's employees- he was trying to cover his tracks in case he killed her.

Now the only problem would be trying to find a place to live...

"Are you sure that this is what you want to do?"

"No, but it's our best bet to not be discovered. Maybe he has his banking info somewhere so I can forge his signature because he still owes me for totaling my car. It's not like I can just take his car or his truck because someone would notice. But, for now, we can use his car to go into town until everything is in order."

"Wait. *What* happened to your car?!" Her grandma demanded.

"He t-boned my car just down the road and flipped it into the ditch. He towed it somewhere, but I don't know where. That's why you couldn't really feel me anymore, because I was dying. Speaking of which, do you know the process of turning someone? Jack never explained to me what he did. I was unconscious the whole time from my injuries."

"I'm not sure I should tell you that..." Her grandma suddenly looked very uneasy.

"Why not?" Kyra asked calmly.

"How do I know you won't use the information for all the wrong reasons?" She eyed her warily.

"Well, I'm going to be spending a lot of time around humans and I don't want to accidentally turn anyone because of my ignorance," she explained. "Could you imagine my mother as a vampire? Yikes." Kyra grimaced at the thought.

Her grandma stared at her, waiting for her to falter. Kyra wasn't lying though. She honestly didn't want to force anyone to go through a shitty transition like she had. Nor did she want to be stuck with her mother for the rest of eternity.

"Okay... I'll tell you, but only if you promise to never turn anyone against their will."

"I promise, gran." She didn't falter or break eye contact as she made her promise.

"The only way for a human to be turned is for them to consume blood from the 'infected.' All vampirism is is a complicated virus with the ability to adapt to new environments and mutate quicker than the human immune system can fight off. Also, if they have an open wound and your blood comes into contact with it, that could turn them as well," her grandmother informed her. Kyra sat there sipping her tea while she processed the new information.

"Seems reasonable enough," she replied, but in her head she was saying, *'great, I might as well have herpes or Aids at this point'*.

Kyra finished her tea and got up out of the living room chair. "I'm going to start going through the office to see if I can find anything. I know you're probably exhausted, so when you're ready, the guest room is next to the bathroom. Goodnight, gran." Kyra bent down and kissed her grandma's cheek and gave her a light hug before leaving the room.

Her aloof behavior probably freaked out her grandmother,

but Kyra wanted to take advantage of feeling numb so she could get some things done. Plus, she no longer needed sleep, but her grandma was human, with human needs.

The office was quite massive compared to the bedrooms. It was the only room in the house that Jack hadn't shown her. No wonder! There were six different monitors, five of which were showing nearly every inch of the property. None of them were facing the upper barn or the front of the house. Kyra would have to go back through the footage later to make sure that her and her grandma were nowhere on it. But, right now, she needed to focus on finding anything linking her to Jack.

Even though the room was quite big, there wasn't much floor space because of all the filing cabinets and multiple desks.

For the next ten hours, Kyra went through every inch of the office, including the past forty-eight hours of camera footage. Kyra was grateful to the fact that she would never have to sleep again. While she was going through Jack's desk, she found a check already made out to her for five grand. Clearly Jack was already planning on paying her back, but that didn't make him a good person.

Thankfully, there was no footage of her or her grandmother. It was like Jack wanted to make sure there was no proof she had ever been there. She shuddered at the thought. Maybe he was trying to keep their kind safe, but Kyra got the feeling that he was trying to cover his tracks because he was already planning on killing her... It's not like there was anything stopping him until her grandmother showed up, becoming a potential witness and another person he'd have to dispose of.

Fifteen

CHAPTER FIFTEEN

Saturday, November 2nd, 2019
_10:36pm_

I'm beginning to think that reality doesn't actually exist. What started out as me believing I was human, turned into a surreal nightmare of events. Who even knows what's real anymore?

After I met with Jack down in the barn, I became violently ill from the sight and smell of the ranch hand's blood. According to Jack, I might still be human after all. Turns out he was wrong. A few hours later, we made a trip into town so I could pack up my things at my parent's house.

On the way back, I began to desiccate and we <u>barely</u> made it back to the house before I died. So, the going theory, once again, was that I was a vampire- a really crappy one at that.

Not long after that, the doorbell rang and there stood my grandmother in all her furious glory. She filled me in on the truth about what's been happening to me. Turns out that I wasn't even

105

human to begin with... I was- hold on to your britches- a <u>witch</u>. A fucking <u>witch</u>! It does make a lot more sense now, but that didn't change the fact that I still wanted to be a vampire.

My grandmother wasn't happy about it at all, but, at the end of the day, the decision was mine to make. She left to get the ingredients for a couple spells but didn't say when she'd be back, so I went down to the barn to help Jack clean up. When I got there, he was acting very off, like he was mad at me for something. He stormed off and went back up to the house so I followed him. He was giving off a very strange vibe and (at the time) I couldn't quite put my finger on it.

When I got up to the house, I heard Jack in his office so I figured I'd let him cool off for a bit and I got to work cleaning my bathroom. The clothes that I had worn for several days straight while I was chained up in the barn were still on the floor. They were so nasty that I had to throw them away, which really sucked because I lost my favorite pair of jeans that I thought of as my 'lucky jeans'. Not like it matters anymore since I grew a couple of inches. I went from being 5'2" to 5'5" literally overnight.

Oddly enough, that wasn't the only part of my appearance that changed. My hair turned a slightly deeper shade of red and I'd swear it grew several inches too. My eyes also changed colors- well, slightly anyway. They went from an olive green to a jade green. My freckles on my nose and cheeks got slightly darker, whereas the ones on my arms and shoulders lightened up. I don't know if I'll keep changing or be frozen in time like the <u>Twilight</u> vampires. I'm just glad I don't fucking sparkle. Weirdos.

I want to try and find other vampires, ones that have been around for a while. I would ask Jack for help, but he had to be removed from the equation. After I finished cleaning my bathroom, Jack was still in his office so I went to my room and started researching everything

I could find on both witches and vampires. Several hours later, he came into my room, bringing me a glass of blood before dinner.

Apparently, he had been doing some research of his own, but something told me that he wasn't being honest so I kept pressing him. Then he started laying on the guilt trip (his own guilt) and tried to make me feel guilty for what he did to me. And, like the idiot I was, I totally fell for it, just like I fell for him. I thought that by kissing him I could prove to him that I forgave him.

Looking back now, I can clearly see how he was constantly manipulating me. I just wish I could've seen through his bullshit before that moment.... When our lips touched, what I saw shook me to my core and I was so terrified that my instant reaction was to protect myself. My mind was flooded with images of mangled corpses covered in blood, but it wasn't just images... It was like I was Jack himself and I could feel everything he felt. I saw into the mind of a cold-blooded serial killer...

I had to play it cool, but it didn't do me any good because Jack knew what I had seen. What I didn't know at the time was that one of his 'abilities' was the power of manipulation, but he could also see the general, basic thoughts of his 'prey.'

Jack didn't try to kill me, so I asked him if he was going to, but he said he wasn't sure because he actually <u>did</u> love me. (As if psychopaths have the ability to love.) I played along and made it clear to him that I just wanted things to go back to normal, like how it was before we kissed. He made the mistake of trusting me so easily because, as we talked, I was sipping on the glass of blood and vaguely forming a plan.

When Jack turned around to leave the room, I smashed my glass across the back of his head, stunning him. He fell to the floor and I picked up a shard of glass and stabbed him in the neck. I pinned him to the ground, my knee on his back, and I drank every last drop of blood as he twitched under me. It seemed like the whole incident was over within seconds.

A few seconds later, I started to finish my transition- just in time for my grandmother to arrive. I can't even imagine what would've happened had she shown up several minutes sooner. I was in so much shock that it took a while for me to fully realize what I had done. I know I shouldn't feel guilty about killing him, but how else am I supposed to feel? He was still a person- an evil, sick person- but still a living, breathing creature. I never wanted to kill anyone, but it was either him or me- there was no doubt about that. Who knows how many people I saved by putting an end to Jackson Hastings? At least now he can never hurt anyone ever again.

The only problem now is, what do I do now? It's not like I can stay here in Jack's house and ignore his dead body on my bedroom floor forever and hope that no one comes looking for him. When he's missed a few shifts at work and no one can get ahold of him, someone's bound to show up looking for him. I have no clue when he was supposed to be back from "vacation" so gran and I will have to leave as soon as possible.

My grandma and I have spent the past two days trying to find anything that could link me to Jack or his house. We even came up with a plan for once we burn down the house. The people in town that saw us together, if they call the cops and I get brought into the station, I'm going to tell them that Jack and I were secretly dating. I'll tell them that we kept it a secret because he was the paramedic that showed up to my 'incident' at work and he didn't want to get in trouble with his superiors.

Then I'll tell them that he brought up having kids way too early on in the relationship and he was wanting something more serious, which was the opposite of what I wanted, so I walked away. I'll say that we ended on good terms because I still love him, but I wanted *more time to work on myself before being tied down.*

I won't go into more detail unless they specifically ask because telling them everything and rambling on can also be seen as an admission of guilt. I'm hoping that no one will remember me but, with my new looks, that's highly doubtful. If I <u>do</u> get called down to the police station, I'll have to hide this journal where it can't be found because I'd be locked up in the nut house. It's going to be really difficult to keep myself out of jail. Technology is so advanced now that it's pretty hard to get away with murder.

That night, after I killed Jack, I checked into a hotel so I would have an alibi. Then the next morning I moved my things back into my parent's house. My mum and I had a little sit-down and I told her I knew about her keeping my condition from me. She didn't apologize, but she did tell me why she did it. According to her, she had scheduled for me to have surgery. She knew I'd be anxious and scared for a few weeks, so she made the decision to keep it from me until the day before the surgery. Not that I believed her motives whatsoever.

To be honest, I understand where she was coming from, but I still would have preferred to know the truth. That still didn't explain why she was so mad at me and treated me like I was crazy. I asked her about it and she got really quiet, so I asked her again. She looked like she was either scared of me, or whatever she had to tell me was so bad that she was scared of what my reaction would be. It was the first time I had ever seen my mother show any emotion beside anger or irritation.

Turns out that my mum has a half-brother. That brother was put up for adoption a couple of years before she was born and her mum (my grandma) never told her about him. When my mum was in high school, she started dating a guy and she lost her virginity to him. Only that, a few weeks later she found out she was pregnant with me, so they went to their parents to tell them the bad news.

As soon as my gran saw my mum's boyfriend, she tried convincing my mum to abort me. Of course, my mum got defensive and they got in a huge argument. That was when gran told her that her boyfriend was actually her half-brother.

My mum started crying as she told me the story.

When she realized what I would be, she tried to kill herself, but gran gave her another option. On the next full moon, gran took my mum to a secret shrine for the goddess Freya and offered a sacrifice. They begged Freya to make sure I was born 'normal' and not have any birth defects.

Clearly, it worked, but they had no clue what Freya had in store for me. Since gran had blocked my powers after I was born, I didn't know anything about magic. But all that magic had to go somewhere, so it went to gran. Turns out that I could've been the most powerful witch to ever live- had I not become a vampire instead. I honestly don't think I'd have been able to handle having all that power. I'm barely responsible enough to take care of my siblings and myself, so there is no way I would be able to handle all of that while having Gandalf level of magic.

Then, earlier today, gran did the spell to unblock my powers. It was such an odd feeling that I started crying. It was like an emotional, static charged tsunami wave that I felt from the top of my head down to the tips of my toes. I know it's only been a few hours, but I thought something would happen the second my powers were returned. Maybe nothing will actually happen, it's not like I've been practicing magic my whole life.

Apparently, I never actually lost my magic when I finished my transition, they had all been transferred to gran for safe keeping until my transition was over.

I was hoping that gran would stick around for a while to help *train me, but her travel visa is going to be expiring soon so she'll have to fly back home soon. It'll be a while before I'm ready to hop on a crowded plane and fly halfway across the world, surrounded by hundreds of humans. Maybe after a few months or so I'll be up for it, but, in the meantime, I'm going to end this here. I have to get back home to keep up appearances.*

Hopefully tomorrow won't be the day I go to jail for murder...

CHAPTER SIXTEEN

Over the next several days, Kyra and her grandma had gone through Jack's entire house looking for any evidence of his stalking. They even made appearances in town with the rest of Kyra's family in an attempt to strengthen their alibi. Mrs. Walsh was completely unaware of everything that happened with Jack. All she knew was that she once again had Kyra right under her thumb.

Kyra and her grandmother had come up with a story to explain to her mother about why gran was in the States. They told her that Kyra had called her grandmother the morning after she had 'moved out.'

Kyra told her mom that her grandma could tell how upset she was and decided to fly over to support her. Mrs. Walsh wasn't too happy about being made out to be the bad guy, but she knew she had been in the wrong. They had actually had a very mature conversation, which surprised Kyra. It was probably only because she was trying to save face in front of her own mother so she wouldn't know what kind of momster she really was.

While growing up, Kyra's mom would blow up whenever Kyra voiced her own opinions if they didn't line up with her own beliefs. She would constantly gaslight Kyra and belittle her, making her feel like a waste of space. The typical behavior of a narcissistic parent.

Kyra was still going to therapy, because it was more important now than ever. She could easily hurt someone if she were to lose her temper and that's something she couldn't afford right now, not when people were beginning to become suspicious.

Jack's work had been calling his house several times a day for the past two days. They didn't have much time left until someone was bound to come investigating. Kyra and her grandma had decided it would be better not to burn the house down because there was no way Jack's body could burn enough unless they used an accelerant, which would point right at it being arson- making it obvious that he had been murdered. Then the cops would be busting her door down.

Kyra was fairly certain that Jack had talked about her at work, but she had no way of finding out without being suspicious. The only thing she *could* do is make sure she has an airtight alibi. That included not leaving town on an extended trip halfway around the world. She'd give it a couple of months for things to die down before she left for Ireland.

For now, Kyra planned on keeping her head down and sticking to the shadows. She had a really bad feeling about the whole situation, like she was totally screwed. Maybe it was her guilt over killing someone.

Kyra was sitting in her room nearly a week after killing Jack. She had been going about her life, which meant continuing her therapy sessions and going to job interviews. It was getting easier to pretend like nothing was wrong, but she didn't think her therapist was convinced. She had to tread lightly so she wouldn't end up in either a straight jacket or a jail cell.

Today was the day that Meghan was supposed to be released from jail, but Kyra wasn't worried about that anymore. If Meghan tried to hurt her, Kyra now had an advantage and could easily remove Meghan from existence. She hoped that Meghan would move on with her life and forget all about her, but that was very unlikely. The last time Kyra had seen her, it was clear that she wasn't going to give up easily. Kyra needed to come up with a plan because she couldn't hide from her forever, especially since she really needed a job, and it's really hard to hide from someone when you work in customer service.

Kyra had gotten several interviews and she was sure that she was going to get a call back from every single one. That wasn't cockiness, that was confidence. At each interview, Kyra could see the exact moment they decided to hire her. Their whole body language would change and she could hear their heart rate change ever so slightly.

The only problem would be trying to pick which ones to accept because some of them were for the same shifts and offered the same amount of hours. They were all minimum wage jobs, but Kyra didn't really care as long as she was making money again. She also had to account for travel time and 'sleep' time so no one would become suspicious.

During her 'sleep' time, Kyra could get a lot of things done- learn a new language, work online, get a degree online. There were so many options. Plus, once she got a routine down, she'd be so busy that she wouldn't have much time to stress about the Jack situation. In addition, once she had a few degrees and some work experience under her belt, then she could finally afford to move away.

Kyra wanted to move to another state- she just wasn't sure yet as to which one. It wasn't going to be a permanent move because there were so many places that Kyra wanted to see. She was most excited to visit Greece because their culture had always fascinated her. Greek mythology always came so easily to her that sometimes she wondered if she had been Greek in another lifetime. Maybe the magic (no matter how dormant it had been) had been drawing her to places of power.

Every so often, Kyra would get flashes of memories that weren't her own. They seemed so foreign to her, but extremely familiar at the same time. Most of the time they only came to her in dreams but, now that her powers aren't blocked, they came to her all the time. Her own memories had come back to her this morning, but it was too late.

Kyra didn't really see a point in going to the cops now since Meghan is getting out of jail today. Plus, Kyra couldn't risk going to the police station and being arrested herself. There was no way for her to be sure that she'd be able to get away with Jack's murder. Meghan wasn't worth going to jail for. Kyra did want to get back at her though because what Meghan put her through was inexcusable and jail time wasn't a good enough punishment. She knew it wasn't her place to punish Meghan, but she didn't want to wait around for her to do it to someone else.

Maybe Kyra could toy with her and make Meghan constantly have to look over her shoulder, wondering when Kyra would strike the final blow. Even *that* idea didn't do anything for her.

She just wanted to completely forget about Meghan and move on with her life. Kyra deserved happiness so she planned to put everything negative behind her and focus on a positive future. Which meant getting a job and going back to school, *and* training to be the best vampire she possibly can be.

The next day:

When Kyra 'woke up' this morning, her abilities still hadn't manifested, but she had a feeling bubbling in her gut that she couldn't explain. The feeling wasn't a good one. Kyra felt like something really bad was coming, but she had no clue when or where it would manifest. Thankfully her severe anxiety was gone, but that didn't mean she no longer felt anxious. Whatever bad thing was coming, it was going to be something really big-something that was going to kill a lot of people. Kyra shoved that feeling down and got out of bed to join her family for breakfast.

During breakfast, Kyra's phone began to ring and she excused herself to take the call. It was one of the pharmacy clerk jobs that she had applied for a few days before. They wanted her to come in later today for an interview and she agreed enthusiastically. Kyra went back to the dining room to tell her family the good news.

"I have an interview later!" Kyra exclaimed as she sat back down at the table.

"That's wonderful, dear!" Her grandmother replied.

"What job?" Her mother asked skeptically.

"One of the pharmacy clerk positions at *Wholesale Drug*. I'm gonna go get ready and prepare some notes for the interview." Kyra hurriedly got up from the table and put away her dishes before her mom could interject, then went to her room to get her things ready for her to take a shower. That was the first thing on her to-do list because her hair always took hours to dry and she didn't want to show up to the interview with sopping wet hair- that would be very unprofessional of her.

Kyra hated blow drying her hair because it always made her hair really frizzy and she wasn't much of a girly-girl to know how to do her hair and makeup. Basically, all she ever wore was mascara and either chapstick or lip gloss. Whenever she had tried wearing more makeup in the past, it had felt as if she had smeared mud on her face. It didn't look much better either. She used to spend hours watching makeup tutorials online and still couldn't figure it out so she gave up.

Even though it was only seven-thirty in the morning and Kyra could've used her vamp speed to get ready, she didn't want to risk her family catching her. She didn't want to scare them or have them find out the truth and shun her. Maybe someday she could tell them one by one when she thought they would be able to handle it. She'd probably start with her sister and then tell her mother. Kyra didn't plan on telling her brother because he liked to gossip with his friends a lot and she couldn't take the risk that he would tell them her secret.

Kyra got the feeling that her mother already knew, or was suspicious because it wasn't like Kyra could hide her sudden change in appearance. She noticed her mom scrutinizing each bite of food she put in her mouth, like she was expecting Kyra to throw up. If that was the case, Kyra wasn't too worried because she could survive on human food for as long as she needed to to avoid suspicion. She was thankful for that little fact because she'd die if she couldn't have chocolate or pizza anymore.

Kyra's absolute favorite food- above cornbread- was pizza because there were so many kinds and topping possibilities that she could never get tired of eating it. Sometimes she would try and make her own so she could experiment with the ingredients. She found that she really liked pepperoni and pineapple on five cheese pizza. The sweetness from the pineapple balanced out the saltiness of the cheese and pepperoni. All of that on a super thick, fluffy crust made her mouth water just thinking about it.

She was in the shower when these thoughts were running through her head and her stomach began to ache with hunger. Even though she had just eaten breakfast, cereal only got her so far. When she was still human, she'd typically be hungry again within an hour of breakfast. Now that she was a vampire, who knew how long human food would satiate her hunger. Kyra promised herself that, once her interview was over, she'd go grab a pizza and maybe hang out with one of her friends. Well, her one and only friend that is.

Kyra hadn't seen her best friend Thomas in a while and she figured she owed him a visit since she had 'bailed' on him the week before. Kyra and Thomas had been friends for as long as she could remember and they always did everything together. They even confided in each other so there were never any secrets between them. Now there were several massive secrets that she couldn't tell him for his own safety.

Thomas had always been by her side as her friend, but Kyra sometimes wondered if they could ever be more than just friends. She thought about asking him many times, but she worried about what that would do to their friendship. She was also scared of being rejected. From what she could tell, Thomas had never shown any romantic feelings towards her, not even a hint of feelings.

Now that she had literally all the time in the world, she decided to shoot her shot. Who knows, maybe he's been in love with her the whole time and was waiting for her to make the first move. They were both really shy around other people, but when they were together they were both very loud and outgoing. It was like they needed each other to be confident and comfortable with themselves, so one would think they'd make a great couple...

They had been friends for so long that Kyra was worried that they wouldn't be able to change their mindset from friends to romantic partners. Her family already thought of Thomas as family so they probably wouldn't be surprised if they were to start dating. Kyra loved Thomas- more than most people because he was the only person who never called her crazy when her anxiety would overwhelm her. He was also the one who brought her back from the dark ledge when she no longer felt like living.

Thomas was the only person who was ever truly there for Kyra and she loved him for that. He never judged her or made her feel like a crazy person like everyone else did. He was the one who had pushed her to get the job at the restaurant even though her anxiety was telling her not to because she'd have to work with the public. Thomas was there when she filled out the online application and then went clothes shopping with her so she could buy an outfit for her interview. He even drove her to the interview since she didn't have her own car yet.

When Kyra came out of that interview with a grin on her face, they went and got dinner to celebrate her getting the job on the spot. She had been anxious for nothing, but Thomas had never said a word about it and did his best to distract her during the days leading up to the interview- even though he knew she had nothing to worry about.

Thomas was the person she confided in every time she had an issue with Meghan or her mother. He kept convincing her to get a new job, but she was making so much just from her tips that she was able to buy a car, plus put extra money in savings. Kyra figured that's why Meghan hated her so much because she made more money than her even though Meghan made more an hour because she was a supervisor. It's not like Kyra would rub it in her face, but they did work a lot of the same shifts so she could see for herself how much Kyra was making in tips.

Because he was able to make her forget about everything with Meghan, Thomas was her favorite person in the whole world, even though she hadn't been treating him as such lately. She has a lot of work ahead of her if she's going to mend their friendship.

CHAPTER SEVENTEEN

Kyra pulled herself out of her head to focus on getting ready for her interview. She still had her slacks from her interview at the restaurant, but she had to hem them because they were slightly too long. Now she just had let out the hem and they'd be the perfect length. It shouldn't take her more than twenty minutes to fix, but she wanted to leave enough time to go to the store in case she messed up and had to get another pair of slacks.

If she passed the interview- which she was fairly certain she would- she'd need a whole new wardrobe because all the pharmacies had a strict dress code. She'd have to wear slacks and blouses when she was used to wearing jeans and t-shirts. She was grateful that she'd be allowed to wear tennis shoes because she *hated* wearing heels. She would get dizzy because she would feel like she was wearing stilts when she wore only two-inch heels, which wouldn't be very good when starting a new job. She also hated the way her toes would get scrunched up and the sides of her feet would hurt so badly after only an hour or so. Kyra needed to be at her best every day from now on because she desperately needed a job.

Now that Kyra was out of the shower, she spent the next half an hour doing her hair and keeping her fingers crossed that it wouldn't turn into a frizzy mess. She knew she was going to wear her charcoal gray slacks with her pale green blouse, but she had no clue what shoes to wear with it. Basically, all she had were tennis shoes and sandals. She still had her solid black non-slip shoes from working at the restaurant, but she'd have to clean them first because they didn't smell too great. She wouldn't be surprised if they still had food grease on them. She'd be lucky if she could clean them well enough and have them dry in time for her to make it to the interview.

With everything that Kyra now needed to get done, she might have to use her vamp speed if she was going to get to her interview on time. She only had an hour left before she needed to leave for her interview because she wanted to make sure she got there early. The pharmacy was in another town and about thirty minutes away. Kyra sometimes hated living in rural Oregon because of how much distance there was in between each town, but the natural beauty of the state made up for it-most of the time.

Kyra cleaned her shoes in the bathroom tub and scrubbed them with a cleaning toothbrush and wiped them dry with a rag, then she brought them to her room and sprayed the insides with perfume. She set them in front of her bedroom fan and got to work undoing the hems on her slacks, which ended up taking way less time than she thought it would. Kyra hoped that no one would notice her sloppy work when she got to her interview.

Knock, knock.

"Kyra, dear? May I come in?" Her grandmother asked.

"Sure, come on in," she replied. Her grandma opened the door and Kyra could see she had a coffee mug in her hands.

"Here, I made this for you. You need to drink it before your interview. I put something a little extra in it for you," she told her.

"What's in it?" Kyra asked as she sniffed it.

"It's coffee, but I added a couple ounces of blood to it so your mum wouldn't notice. I don't think she's quite ready for that kind of discussion," she explained.

"Good thinking. Thanks, gran," Kyra said with a smile as she gave her grandma a one-armed hug. Kyra took the mug and took a small sip. The warmth and caffeine from the coffee made the blood feel like an electric charge as it hit her tongue. She could feel the warmth spreading through her body as she continued to drink. She felt as if she had been wrapped in a big, fuzzy, heated blanket on a cold, rainy day. Kyra could also feel all the endorphins rushing through her body and she felt happier than she's ever been.

"Feeling better?" Her grandma asked. Kyra nodded as she finished off the last drops. "Good. Just so you know- even though you can survive on human food- the longer you go without blood, the crankier and more dangerous you'll become. And if you go long periods of time without feeding, the next time you feed you could turn into a ripper- like Jackson- and completely lose control," she explained.

"So how often should I be feeding?" Kyra asked cautiously.

"To air on the side of caution, I'd say at least an ounce a day, every day. You can obviously have more than that, but not without risking the blood lust. Consuming a lot of blood on a regular basis and becoming dependent on it can also turn you into a ripper." Kyra stared at her grandma, trying to figure out how she could possibly respond to that.

"A ripper?... Like a monster that can no longer feel anything except the urge to feed and kill?" Kyra questioned. She'd heard the term once or twice on a show called *The Vampire Diaries* that she used to be obsessed with back when she was in high school. Well, more like obsessed with Damon Salvatore that is. Kyra could see past the bad boy behavior and it intrigued her.

"Precisely. Don't worry, my dear. I believe that you are strong enough and smart enough, otherwise I wouldn't have allowed you to become a vampire. You're just going to need to continue to be responsible and never neglect your needs.

In other words, she could never risk slipping up or she could end up killing everyone she's ever loved. *Great...*

"Sounds reasonable enough..." Kyra shrugged. "I have to leave for my interview now. I don't want to be late."

"Drive safe, sweetie." Her grandma gave her a hug and went back downstairs. Kyra grabbed her notes and put them in her purse and put her shoes on. She nearly forgot that she needed to defrost the windows in the car, so it's a good thing she had already planned on leaving extra early. She hadn't had to use the defroster in Jack's car yet, so she wasn't sure how long it would take.

Kyra was on her way to the interview less than ten minutes later and she was still going to get there about fifteen minutes early. She sat in the car for ten minutes or so and jammed out to some music to get herself in the right head-space before going in five minutes early. She had a good feeling about this interview and hopefully she was right because she *really* needed this job... She walked inside and waited in line until she got to the counter.

"Hi, I'm Kyra Walsh. I have an interview with Courtney at ten-thirty." Kyra was suddenly really nervous, but she did her best not to let it show.

"Hi, Kyra. Gimme a sec and I'll go grab her for you," the clerk told her. She seemed really nice. Kyra hoped that there wasn't a negative reason for them needing another clerk, because this one was lovely. Hopefully she was just moving on to something bigger and better, or maybe she was planning on taking a sabbatical or something.

The inside of the pharmacy was starting to get busy already so hopefully they were frequently busy enough that Kyra could get quite a few hours. The more hours, the better, because she really didn't relish the idea of having to work two jobs at the same time. She'd rather work a good number of hours at one singular job, and then do her schooling or hobbies at night.

"Hello, Kyra. I'm Courtney," a woman greeted her as she walked around the counter and shook Kyra's hand. "Let's go into the office and see if you're a good fit for the position." Courtney smiled at her and Kyra felt more at ease as they walked into the office to sit down at the tiny table.

"So, what led you to apply for the clerk position?" She asked Kyra.

"Well, jobs in the medical field are always looking for positions to fill and this was the only way for me to get my foot in the door without any kind of medical degree. I've already begun studying to become a pharmacy technician, but I was hoping to learn by working in a pharmacy and by watching other technicians work as well- as I retain information a lot easier when I'm actively involved," Kyra answered.

"That's actually very smart. Are you taking any classes or are you learning on your own?"

"I'm doing it on my own for now since I missed the window to sign up for the class, but I've been looking into certification courses that are specifically online so I can work during the day and then do my schooling at night. I figured that if I learned a lot on my own time, then once I actually found people to study with, I'd be able to keep up more easily," she answered honestly.

"That is honestly so amazing. That is so good to hear! Next question, do you have reliable transportation for getting to work?" Courtney asked.

"Yes."

She wasn't about to tell her that that could change at any moment.

"What kind of hours are you looking for? I see on your application that you put full time. What do you consider to be full time?"

"I consider forty hours to be full time, but I'm willing to work more than that if needed. I'm even open to working weekends and holidays if needed," Kyra replied.

"That's what I like to hear! But, overtime rarely happens here- especially for the clerk position- and we are closed for all major national holidays. Do you think you'll be able to handle being on your feet for eight to ten hours a day?" Courtney asked. "There will be some occasional shifts where you will have longer hours, but most of your shift will range between four to seven hours depending on the day of the week."

"I know I can. I worked a lot of double shifts at my last job as a waitress and I rarely ever got my breaks. I do have some questions of my own now though- if that's okay."

"Sure, go ahead," Courtney said with a smile.

"If I get the position and I've been here for several months or so, will I still be at minimum wage, or does the wage go up every so often?" She asked.

"That's an excellent question, I'm glad you asked. So, for the first sixty days, you'll be at minimum wage and then it will go up twenty-five cents an hour. Then, once you reach that, you'll stay at that wage unless you become a technician. And as for the hours, I'd start you at twenty-five hours per week until you've learned enough to be on your own. Would that work for you?" Courtney explained to her.

"Of course!" Kyra replied. "Is there any specific kind of dress code?"

"What you have on right now is perfect. The only rules we have are you have to be wearing non-slip shoes and have your hair pulled back during the shift," Courtney explained.

"That works for me," Kyra said. She was beyond excited at this point because the interview was going way better than she thought it would.

"When would you like to start?" Courtney asked.

"As soon as possible. The sooner, the better," Kyra laughed.

"What about right now? I mean, you're already dressed for the job so why not? I mean, if that's okay with you."

"That would be great!" Kyra texted her mom quickly letting her know that she got the job on the spot and would let her know later on when she'd be home before following after Courtney. Also, that way Kyra wouldn't be expected to make dinner for the family tonight and she's given her mom enough time to come up with a different plan for dinner.

"So, since you're starting at eleven today, you'll be working until closing at six. You'll be working with Fiona today and learning from her. She'll show you what to do in your down time, so have fun and I'll check in with you later." Courtney walked away and Kyra couldn't get the huge grin off her face. She had to focus on what Fiona was saying and not let herself get distracted by the fact of how easily she got the job. She'd call Thomas on her lunch break and see if he was available to meet her for dinner when she got off work, then she'd text her mom back and let her know what was going on.

CHAPTER EIGHTEEN

"Hey, Thomas. Are you busy?" Kyra asked.

"Not at all, what's up?" He replied.

"Do you want to get dinner around seven later?" She asked.

"Sure! What did you have in mind?"

"How about Mexican food? I've been craving nachos lately," she chuckled.

"Works for me! I'm actually available right now too if you wanted to grab lunch- my treat," he suggested. Kyra felt bad at that last part. It should be her treating *him* to a meal, not the other way around- especially not after how horrible of a friend she'd been over the past few weeks.

"I'm actually at work on my lunch break right now," she told him.

"Wait, what? You have a job? Since when?! And you didn't bother to tell me?"

"Whoa, slow down there!" She laughed. "I actually just

started this morning. I came in for an interview and got the job on the spot. I'm so excited!" She exclaimed. She was sitting in her car, eating the sandwich she had just gotten from the *Subway* down the road.

"For real?! That's great! I'm so happy for you, Kyra!" He exclaimed.

"I was actually going to tell you at dinner tonight," she laughed. "There's actually something else I wanted to talk to you about, but I'd rather do it in person." She tried not to let it show in her voice, but she was nervous about talking to him.

"Hey, is everything okay? You kinda dropped off the map last week and I couldn't get ahold of you," he said.

"Yeah, my grandmother showed up for an unannounced visit and things at home have been hella crazy. My grandma spilled the tea on a few major family secrets… I'm still trying to wrap my head around it all. I'll tell you about it later during dinner," she reassured him.

"Are you sure you're okay? You sound a little… different," He asked.

"I'm sure," she chuckled. "Don't worry, I'll be over as soon as I get off work. My lunch break is almost over and I still gotta text my mum and let her know not to wait up for me tonight," she explained.

"No problem. See you later."

"Bye," she replied. Kyra hung up and immediately texted her mom.

Kyra walked back into work, excited to finish her first day at her new job and to see her best friend after work. She planned on giving herself a few days before looking for a second job so she could have some time to find her new routine.

During her shift, Kyra had made the decision to go ahead

and try to find a second job because, with only getting around twenty-five hours a week, it's going to take her *years* to save up enough to move back to Ireland. Plus, the more money she can save up now, the longer she'll have to look for a job once she's there and settled in.

The rest of the shift flew by so quickly that Kyra couldn't believe it was already over. She had spent the day learning everything she could and getting to know her new co-workers in her down time. So far, everyone was really kind to her which she greatly appreciated. It was a fairly small pharmacy, so there were only a total of seven employees- including herself. There were only three pharmacy technicians and Kyra had spent a good portion of the shift watching them work- locking away all that new information in her brain for a later date.

If she studied long and hard enough, Kyra figured she could take the certification test within only a month or two. She wasn't quite sure about that whole process yet, so she'd give herself a week or so before asking her new co-workers.

Who knows, maybe now that she was stronger, faster, and smarter (hopefully), maybe she'd change her mind about becoming a pharmacy tech. It's not like she doesn't have an eternity to do whatever she wants.

Kyra got off work right at six and drove the twenty-five minutes to Thomas's house. They both grew up in the same small town and lived only a street away from each other. They spent so much time at each other's houses that they no longer needed to knock. Kyra would come home from work and Thomas would either be in her room or hanging out with her siblings.

Thomas was an only child, but, over time, Kyra's siblings had begun to feel more like his own. He would sometimes help out with the kids when Kyra's parents weren't home so she could get a few extra hours on her pay checks. She was sure her parents knew, but they trusted Thomas enough to let him be there alone with the kids. Thomas had even gone to Ireland with Kyra and her family the last time they went. Kyra and Thomas had gone off by themselves to explore when her family wanted to stay at the hotel.

Once Kyra got to Thomas's house, she sat in her car for a few minutes out of pure nervousness. She knew he'd immediately notice the difference in her appearance and she still didn't know how to explain it without telling him the truth, so she decided to start with the situation with her parents and then go from there. Would he hate her once he knew the whole truth?

Only one way to find out, she thought to herself as she got out of the car and walked into the house. She found him in the kitchen getting their dinner ready. He had his back to her and hadn't heard her come in so she stood there watching him.

He looked different to her now as she looked at him with her new and improved eyesight. How had she never noticed how attractive he really was? She had always found him attractive, but never *this* attractive. When had he slimmed down and become fit? Kyra could see the muscles straining against the fabric of his form fitting, long-sleeved shirt and had to hold back her gasp. He was one of the most beautiful men she had ever seen. It was a wonder that he was still single... She felt her cheeks get hot as she continued checking him out.

Was he really not interested in someone? Or was he hung up on someone he couldn't have? Either way, she still had a chance to tell him how she felt. She'd tell him before she headed home later so she wouldn't ruin their dinner, because she really did want to tell him about everything that's happened over the past couple of weeks. He was still her best friend after all. Hopefully, once he knew everything, he wouldn't walk out of her life. She didn't think she'd be able to handle that as well- not with her life being a walking circus these days.

"Hey, stranger," Kyra said quietly. Thomas nearly jumped out of his skin.

"For fuck's sake, Kyra!" He screamed. "I didn't hear you come in," he said as he turned to face her. He froze and Kyra could see a bunch of emotions and questions cross his face. The last one being fear.

Shit.

CHAPTER NINETEEN

"What the hell happened to you? You look so… different."

"Is it really that much of a difference?" She asked, knowing full well how big of a change it was. She didn't dare move or breathe as he stared at her with fear and confusion in his eyes.

"What are you? You're not my Kyra…" He looked terrified.

"Tommy, you should sit down… It's a *very* long story. I'm still me, I'm still the Kyra you've always known. I'll explain everything as soon as you sit down." He flinched when she moved out of the kitchen doorway so he could go around her. She cringed inwardly as her stomach dropped. He hated her… The last person to stay by her side not only hated her, but was now terrified to death of her.

"Are you going to kill me?" He asked. Kyra could hear his heart racing and she couldn't fight back the tears.

"Of course not! Thomas, I'd *never* hurt you!" She promised. He took a seat on the couch and Kyra sat on the floor across the room from him with her back against the wall.

"Well, I'm listening," he said cautiously. She felt so bad about how terrified he was so she started from the *very* beginning, starting with the incident at work. The more she talked, the more his heart rate slowed. She wasn't sure if it was because of her new voice entrancing him, or if he was beginning to trust her again.

Once she got to the part about killing Jack, she glossed over the details as to not frighten him even further- she didn't think his heart would be able to handle that. Then, when she told him about how she was actually a witch before she was turned, he started laughing hysterically.

"Why are you laughing?" She asked, shocked by his sudden outburst.

"So, let me get this straight. You expect me to believe that you're a *vampire* who used to be a *witch*? Are you fucking kidding me? How stupid do you think I am?! Clearly you don't trust me enough to tell me the truth. I'd like you to leave," he demanded.

"I *am* telling you the truth though!" She looked him straight in the eye as she focused on the blood pulsing through his body. She smiled at him and watched his face as he saw her fangs descend.

"Holy shit!" He screamed in horror. His face turned so pale that Kyra questioned whether that had been the right thing to do. Her intent wasn't to shock him, but instead prove that what she had said was in fact the truth. She remained on the floor across the room from him while she retracted her fangs.

His eyes never left her face and Kyra could see the horror and betrayal in his eyes. Had she just ruined their entire fifteen-year friendship? She was mentally kicking herself, wishing she hadn't called him earlier and made plans to hang out. Clearly, Thomas wanted her gone, so she got up slowly and headed to the front door.

"Don't leave…" Kyra turned around and saw Thomas still sitting on the couch, but he was crying. Out of all the years they had been friends, Kyra had only seen Thomas cry maybe twice, she she wasn't quite sure how to react.

She sat back down slowly as not to spook him.

"Hey, please don't cry. Talk to me, tell me what's going through your head," she pleaded softly. Were his tears from her scaring him?

"I don't want to lose you, Kyra. There's no way you'd ask for something like this to happen. I was so rude to you… Will you please forgive me?" He apologized. "I can't lose you…" Another tear fell as he choked out that last word.

"Thomas, I'll always forgive you! There is nothing for me to forgive. This is all my fault and I'm so sorry for not telling you sooner."

Her heart felt like it were shattering more with each tear that dripped down his cheeks. She wished more than anything that things could go back to the way they were before. She felt so stupid in this moment for ever thinking that becoming a vampire was the best thing for her to do. She should have listened to her grandmother…

She slowly got up from the floor and made her way over to the opposite end of the couch from where he was sitting. The distance between them was killing her inside. Kyra kept scooting closer until she was close enough to hug him.

He flinched slightly as she put her hand on his. She froze. Kyra couldn't risk rushing and causing him even more emotional and psychological harm.

As she touched him, she was flooded with his true feelings for her and immediately felt her cheeks heat up. It wasn't out of embarrassment, but surprise. He's loved her since the day they met in the second grade...

Kyra then leaned in and kissed his forehead, cradling his face in her hands. She pulled away and looked him in the eyes.

"I love you, Thomas." She teared up. It took a moment but then a grin broke out across his face as the meaning of her words finally sank in.

"You don't know how long I've been waiting for you to say those words," he grinned.

"Since the day we met in second grade," she replied without thinking.

"Wait, you knew? How long have you known?" He wondered.

"I didn't really. At least not until a few seconds ago when I saw myself through your eyes; I knew instantly."

"What do you mean by that?" He asked.

"One of my new abilities is that I can see people's strongest emotions and memories when I touch them," she explained. "Pretty cool, huh? I didn't start to notice it until this morning when I hugged my gran before I had left for my interview.

"Did you kiss my forehead out of pity?" He asked, his face crumbling.

"Not at all! The reason why I called you earlier was because I was going to confess my feelings for you. I just didn't want it to get in the way of our friendship. I honestly thought you only saw me as a sister."

"I did try for years to see you like that so it would be easier to be by your side, but the harder I tried, the stronger my feelings got. After a while, I got used to just being by your side without any expectations. I tried thinking of myself as being your protector. Knowing you were safe and happy made the feelings a lot more bearable."

"Why didn't you ever tell me how you felt?" Kyra asked.

"I did try a couple of times, but I was interrupted by someone every single time. Do you remember when we were in Dublin and that tourist couple asked us to take their picture for them? That was the last time I tried telling you. By that point, I felt like the universe was either telling me it wasn't the right time, or that we just weren't meant to be."

He let out a long, tortured sigh. Kyra felt so bad for never noticing his feelings for her that she wanted to do something to try making up for a little bit of lost time.

"Can I try something? I don't know if it'll work." Kyra had an idea for something crazy- but she had a gut feeling that that crazy thing might just work in her favor.

"Will it hurt?..." He asked skeptically.

"I don't think so, but I've never tried this before, so no promises."

"I guess so," he agreed skeptically. She took his right hand and placed it on her heart, then put his left hand on her right temple. She then mirrored that with her own hands.

"Okay, now relax and let your mind go blank," she instructed. "Now, on the count of three, tell me if you see anything." Kyra took a deep breath and put her energy behind her memories and directed them towards his being as she counted to three. She was showing him her car accident and the process of her turning because she knew he wouldn't be able to guess the details very easily since she had been unconscious for most of it.

"I feel cold... Ah! My whole body hurts! Wait, now I feel warm. I feel high... Did you drug me?! Ahhh! Kyra! Please.

Stop! No more, please! I don't want to see any more!" Thomas sobbed. Kyra didn't stop. Instead, she showed him the memory from very early this morning when she realized she had feelings for him. Then she showed him what she had seen when they touched and she lingered on an image of their faces together.

Kyra let go and they both opened their eyes. She stayed silent while she waited for Thomas to process everything. She could see that she had overwhelmed him, so she scooted back over to the other end of the couch. They stared at each other for what felt like hours to Thomas, but Kyra knew it had only been a few minutes.

"What was that last part about? Why did you show me my own memory?" He asked quietly, barely above a whisper.

"I was showing you the way I saw it in your mind and that I felt the same way. Or did I misinterpret your memory?" She wondered.

"No, you got it right. But why did you show me more after I asked you to stop?" He asked accusingly. That trust Kyra had just worked so hard to build back was now gone again and she only had herself to blame.

"I didn't want those bad images to be the only thing you see when you look at me. They were scary enough for me when I had to go through it, but I'm here with you and I'm okay. Life is always moving forward and I don't want to be stuck in the past, constantly worrying about whether or not I made the right choices. I want to move forward with you and make more happy memories to smother out the bad ones," she explained.

"Are you immortal?" He asked.

"Yes," she sighed. "And, yes, I can go out in the sun- just not for very long. The more I'm out in the sun or the more I exert myself, the more frequently I have to feed," she explained.

"Do you want to kill me?" He asked. Kyra could hear his heart falter and skip a beat as he spoke.

"Nope. I never got the blood lust," she shrugged. "Plus, I'd never do anything to hurt you or my family." He still didn't look convinced.

"How can I believe you?"

"Do you seriously think I could've made it the whole day at work without killing any of my co-workers if I were lying? The pharmacy is open to the public, so don't you think someone would have noticed if there were dead people and blood everywhere?" She asked him.

"True… If that really is the truth, is that the same for other vampires then?" He asked cautiously.

"I don't think so. The only other vampire I've met was Jack, so I don't have anyone else to ask. As far as I know, I'm a bit of an oddity in the supernatural world."

"Is that all?" He laughed nervously.

"Not quite. Actually… do you remember earlier today when I told you that my grandma spilled some major family secrets?" She asked.

"Yeah, what about it?" He replied.

"Well… Turns out that my dad isn't just my dad… He's also my uncle. As in my mom's half-brother…" She looked down at her hands, not able to meet his gaze.

"Wait, what?!" He exclaimed. "So, your mom's half-brother is also your biological father?!" He was beyond shocked.

"Yup… He was put up for adoption a couple of years before my mom was born. He was adopted by a family in their area. So, when they grew up, they ended up going to the same secondary school. They didn't know they were related until after my mum got pregnant with me and they had to tell their parents," she explained. Thomas was quiet as he let that information sink in.

"What about your siblings?" He asked.

"Bryton and Chloe are both adopted. They don't know the truth about my dad-uncle and my mum wants to keep it that way because it would upset them too much if they found out," she told him.

"Is that all?" He chuckled.

"Not quite…" This time she looked up but had to quickly look away.

"There's more?!" He asked, exasperated.

"Believe me, I wish there wasn't," she sighed. "When my mum told gran that she was pregnant, gran took her to a sacred place and asked the goddess Freya for help. They weren't sure she would help, but they wouldn't know anyway until after I was born. Freya used her magic to help create me… I am technically what they call a tri-brid. I am part vampire, witch, and goddess. According to my grandmother, I am the most powerful being in the world… Surprise." She chuckled nervously.

Thomas's jaw dropped. He was so shocked, he couldn't think of what to say. Kyra was sure she just fried his brain.

Maybe I should have waited to tell him that part, Kyra thought to herself.

"Are you okay?…" She asked after a few moments of deafening silence. He was massaging his temples and had his eyes closed. Had she broken his mind? Kyra got up from her end of the couch and sat next to him. She had no clue what she was doing, but she had a feeling that was drawing her towards him. She placed one hand on his forehead and the other on the back of his head.

Kyra closed her eyes and focused on pulling the warmth from

her happiest memories and directed it towards him to help ease his mind. She could feel the tension leave his heart and mind and she pulled away. Kyra felt tired as if she had just completed a quarter mile sprint. She scooted away from him again, but only a few inches this time.

"Thank you," he whispered.

"How're you feeling?" She asked after a moment of silence.

"Extremely tired," Thomas replied. "Do you mind if I go to bed?" He asked.

"Sure, no problem. I'll go put dinner away and clean up the kitchen before I leave," she told him.

"Okay, thanks. I'll see you later, goodnight," he said as he got up off the couch and walked out of the living room.

"Goodnight…" She whispered.

Kyra watched him walk down the hall to his bedroom and close the door behind him. She got a sinking feeling- like he had just shut the door on their friendship and any possibility of a relationship. She'd give him a couple days to process everything before she came around again.

Kyra cleaned up the kitchen and then walked out the front door, locking it behind her. She'd had a key to his house since they were kids, just as he had a key to her house.

Thomas had inherited his parent's house when they retired to Florida two years ago. Since then, he had managed to remodel the entire house and Kyra was beyond proud of him. He had turned a 1960s ranch house into a modern beauty. Kyra helped him with painting and landscaping on her down time and they had a lot of fun with it.

They would spend hours cracking jokes and listening to music while they worked on the house. Their favorite song was *Burning Up (Fire)* by *BTS* because they were always sweating while they worked- they thought it was punny. Kyra really missed those days... She hoped to see more days like those in the future- especially with Thomas by her side. If he decided that he wanted to stay in her life, it wouldn't be an eternity because Kyra couldn't bear the thought of making Thomas go through what she had to. Not to mention, she had promised her grandmother that she would never turn anyone.

Kyra got back in her car and drove around the corner to her house. She wasn't quite ready to go inside and be interrogated by her mom, so she sat in the car and listened to her music. It was only eight o'clock, so Kyra knew her mom was still awake. If she went inside right now, her mom would be able to tell from one look that something was wrong.

How could she possibly explain that she may have just ruined her one and only friendship? How could she tell her that Thomas was terrified of her without telling her why? The answer was that there was no way, so she reclined her seat and closed her eyes and let the music wash over her. She didn't care that it was freezing cold in the car since it no longer bothered her like it used to.

After an hour, Kyra looked out the window and saw that all the windows in the house were dark. If her mom was waiting to ambush her, she'd just tell her that she dozed off in the car and needed to go to bed. She did work a full shift after all- not that she'd actually sleep once she got to her room.

As soon as she was sure everyone was asleep, Kyra planned on getting her laptop out to start applying for online college courses. If she could get some kind of degree in at least something useful, then she could land a really nice job. She eventually wanted to own her own business so she could choose her own hours and do something she actually found joy in. Not that she knew what that was yet since she was still finding who she is as a person. She'd take a couple of business courses so she could get that degree out of the way while she figured out the type of business she wanted.

Kyra snuck into the house and carefully locked the door as quietly as possible behind her. Thankfully, she had snuck in enough times to know how to avoid the squeaky steps. Now that she had stronger hearing along with night vision, she could easily sneak in and her family would be none the wiser.

It took Kyra less than a minute to make it to her room. She put a rolled-up blanket down on the floor at the bottom of her door so no one would see the light come from her room. She then got to work on the applications. If she used vamp speed, she'd be able to get them done in about an hour, but that would tire her out and her blood supply was already running low. Dangerously low if she was being honest with herself-especially since she hadn't expected to work a full shift, plus use her new powers for a while afterwards.

Kyra had gotten into the habit of going to Jack's house every day to refill her reusable cup with blood from the stockpile of blood bags that he kept in a mini-fridge in his kitchen. She had never hunted before and just the thought of it terrified her. She hadn't learned how to compel people yet, and now that Jack was gone, she had no one to teach her. She'd have to find someone willing to be her test subject so she could practice-but who could she ask? The only people who even knew about her were her grandmother and Thomas- and she wasn't about to test it out on one of her siblings either.

She didn't have to work until noon tomorrow, so she had plenty of time to go to Jack's house and get back before anyone woke up. She decided to leave at three in the morning so that she could be back by four since her mom would be getting up at five for work. Plus, at that time of morning, there wouldn't be any traffic so she could speed. She was going to get more blood this time so she wouldn't have to keep going back and forth to Jack's house.

Instead of filling up her one cup, Kyra planned on taking Jack's mini-fridge of blood and plug it in in her room. She'd shove it into her closet though, so hopefully her mom wouldn't go snooping in her room while she's at work. Her mom had a tendency to do that for as long as she could remember and it always irritated her because it wasn't like she ever went into her mom's room and gone through her things- it's called privacy.

It's not like Kyra ever had anything to hide, but she still liked to have her own private space where she could be herself. But- with everything going on now- she *really* needed to have some privacy. She could only imagine what her mom would think if she found her blood stash. Kyra *could* tell her mom the truth, but why should she?

Mrs. Walsh had never supported Kyra emotionally and she always made Kyra feel like an idiot. So why should she share her new world with her? Kyra felt like she deserved something in her life that could bring her happiness and she didn't want her mom to ruin that.

Kyra ended up leaving way sooner than she had planned because she didn't want to take a chance and have her mom wake up before she got back from Jack's house. There were no other cars out on the road- not even cops- so Kyra made it to his house in basically no time at all.

His house was extra creepy this time of night, especially since she felt like she was being watched. She risked using her vamp speed to get the fridge because she didn't want to have to be in that house any longer than necessary. With no one having been inside for a while, it was just about as cold inside as it was outside- which only added to the creepy factor.

Once she was on her way back home, she drove the speed limit because she wasn't about to risk getting pulled over with a crap ton of blood bags in the car. It wasn't as if she had the ability to talk her way out of it since she still hadn't learned how to compel people- making this the riskiest thing she had ever done.

When she got back home, she used her vamp speed again, for the second time that night, so she wouldn't risk making too much noise. It wasn't even two in the morning by the time Kyra was back in her room and had the mini-fridge plugged in. Now, the hardest part would be rationing what was left of the blood...

If she were to consume the least amount of blood each day, she could probably make it all last two weeks, maybe three. It mainly depended on how often she exerted herself. She'd have to be careful until she could figure out what to do next.

CHAPTER TWENTY

Kyra missed a few human things already, one of which was sleep. If she were able to sleep, she could get a few hours of peace. She missed being able to forget about her worries for at least a few hours and escape to a whole other world of her own making.

At around 2am, Kyra put on a comfy pair of pajamas and crawled into bed with a book. She'd set her book aside every so often to try and make herself sleep, but nothing happened. She felt like she had just had a huge cup of coffee right before bed.

She tossed and turned out of irritation for several hours until she heard her mom's alarm clock go off on the other side of the house. Now Kyra had to try and make it through at least another five hours before it would be an acceptable time to get up for work. She felt exhausted just thinking about it. Maybe she could find a way to meditate enough to completely empty

147

her mind from time to time. It would make the passing of time a lot easier now that she's looking at an eternity of monotonous days.

Kyra could hear her mom making a pot of coffee in the kitchen and soon the smell began to waft into her room. She decided to get up and make breakfast for the two of them. That would give them a few minutes to talk about her new job before her mom had to finish getting ready for work.

"Good morning, mum," Kyra greeted her mother as she entered the kitchen.

"Morning. What time did you get home last night?" She asked.

"Sometime around eight-thirty, but I was so tired that I fell asleep in the car as soon as I got home," she explained.

"How did your first day go?" Her mom asked.

"It was one of the best days ever! The interview went so well that I was hired on the spot. I go in at noon again today to finish my training, then, after that, I'll be working the opening shift Wednesday through Saturday," she told her.

"That's wonderful, dear! What is the pay like?"

Her mother seemed genuinely happy for her, which was abnormal behavior for her. Maybe her mother had finally taken her advice about finding a therapist to talk to.

"It's minimum wage to start out, but it'll go up after I've been there for sixty days. Once I've gotten into a routine, I'll get a second part time job until they can give me more hours at the pharmacy," she told her mom.

"Sounds like an excellent plan," she agreed.

Kyra made them eggs, bacon, and hash browns for breakfast and then cleaned up the dishes while her mom got ready for work. She quietly loaded the dishes into the dishwasher, then poured herself a fresh cup of coffee and brought it to her room.

Once in her room, Kyra locked her door and snuck into her closet. She opened the mini-fridge and grabbed one of the blood bags, pouring some into the sweet, hot coffee. Her mouth began to water and her fangs dropped. After pouring it into her cup, she walked over and unlocked her bedroom door.

The warmth from the coffee made the blood smell fresh. She had to remind herself to be responsible and only consume the bare minimum, but the smell was making it difficult for her to think straight. She hoped that after a while she'd become desensitized to the smell of blood and be able to lengthen the amount of time between feedings.

When Kyra had gotten back from Jack's house earlier this morning, she hadn't had any blood because she wanted to push herself to her maximum limit. Now she was regretting that earlier decision. She wanted to drain every last drop of blood. Instead, she sat back down on her bed and read a book while she slowly sipped her coffee.

Kyra was trying her hardest to focus more on the book than her phone, so she didn't notice when her grandmother got up. It had taken Kyra nearly an hour to read only two chapters because she kept getting distracted by *TikTok*. She'd had it for almost a year now, but she hadn't posted any videos yet because she was afraid of getting bullied.

For the next hour, Kyra went back and forth between reading her book and watching *TikTok*. She *loved* the book side of *TikTok* and she already had a list of over a hundred books she wanted to buy. There were just so many authors on there that it was hard to pick her favorite. She already had a decent collection of books, but she had read all of them multiple times already. Now that it only took her a couple of hours to read a big novel, she'd be able to get through her list in no time at all.

Kyra heard her grandmother coming up the stairs, but she was finally getting into the book and was in the middle of a chapter. She was still reading when her grandma came in her room without knocking. Kyra didn't look up.

"Good morning, Kyra. How was your night?" She asked in a way that Kyra could tell something was up.

"It was boring, as always. Why?" She replied.

"Where did you go off to? I heard you leave in the middle of the night," her grandmother questioned.

"Has my mum left for work yet?" She asked as she used her hearing to search the house.

"Not yet. You didn't answer my question," she pointed out. Kyra put her finger to her lips, motioning for her to keep quiet as she tiptoed over to her closet. She quietly opened the closet door and moved her clothes to one side, exposing the mini-fridge.

"I couldn't keep sneaking to Jack's house every time I need to feed," she whispered.

"How much do you have left?" Her grandma asked.

"Hopefully enough for a couple of weeks or so. That is, as long as I ration it and not use my abilities unless I absolutely have to," she explained.

"What are you going to do after that? Have you even thought about that?" She questioned.

"I honestly have no clue, gran… That's all I've been able to think about for days now," she whispered. "I don't want to hurt anyone… How am I supposed to feed from someone? Jack never got a chance to teach me." Kyra began to feel her anxiety brewing under the surface as the affects from the blood wore off.

"You're just going to have to trust your gut on this I'm afraid," her grandma empathized. "I wanted to remind you that I'm flying back home today, so I won't be here to help you. But, I'm always just a phone call away when you have any questions. You'll have to come visit me once you feel comfortable enough to make it through the long, cramped flight."

"I wish I could go with you today, but I have to stay here for a little while longer and pretend to be normal. At least for a couple of months until the Jack thing blows over," she explained.

"I understand," her grandmother replied.

Kyra regretted the years that she missed out on getting to know her grandma. They were already becoming two peas in a pod and she knew she was going to miss her extremely once she flew back home.

"Hey, gran? Can I ask you something?" Kyra asked.

"Sure, dear. What's on your mind?"

"Over the past couple of days, I've been feeling very off. I keep getting the feeling that something bad is coming. Do you feel it too, or is it just me?" She asked.

"It's not just you. I feel it too. As green witches, we are connected to the earth and every living thing. Humans have become selfish- so selfish that they've destroyed the planet, throwing the world out of balance. Mother nature will be getting her revenge soon enough. I suggest you prepare for the worst, because it's going to take at least a few years for things to normalize again," she told her.

"Prepare how? Like build an underground bunker or something?" Kyra asked in a mocking tone.

"No, nothing like that. I suggest you make sure that you have plenty of food and supplies to last at least six months or so.

You'll have to take care of your mum and the kids- mainly the kids because your mother will be even busier at work for quite some time. I'd suggest for all of you to come back to Ireland but you and your mum have responsibilities here." Her grandma looked scared, which freaked Kyra out because her grandma never showed fear towards anything. Whatever was heading their way, it could be big enough to end up in the history books one day.

Kyra's grandma gave her a hug and went back downstairs to her room, leaving Kyra standing there by herself. She was trying to refrain from drinking more blood as a way to make herself feel better. She knew the blood would give her a temporary high, but then she'd be even closer to having to feed on a human. That would be *very* bad for her, *and* the unsuspecting human.

Her phone buzzed on her bed and her stomach dropped as she saw the message notification from Thomas. This was the moment of truth. Did he still want to be in her life, or did he want to run away screaming? She decided to rip off the band aid and read the message.

She quickly glanced at the message and saw Thomas's apology. She texted him back asking to meet up after the end of her shift.

Kyra set her phone aside and got out her journal to write for a while. It's not like she had anything better to do right now. It was only six-thirty in the morning and she still had another two hours until she took her grandma to the airport, and five hours until she needed to leave for work. She'd get up after a while to make sure her siblings got to school on time since her mom had already left for work.

Once they were off to school, Kyra loaded her grandma's

bags into the car and drove her to the airport. It was a little over an hour drive so Kyra and her grandma rocked out to some music during the long drive. Kyra still had plenty of time before she needed to be to work so she wasn't in a hurry to get back home. She wanted to shop around for an hour before heading back home, but she would need to feed again before work.

CHAPTER TWENTY-ONE

As Kyra was walking back to the car after walking her grandmother to her gate, her phone began buzzing in her back pocket. She didn't recognize the number, but she answered anyway.

"Hello?" She answered.

"Hi. Is this Kyra Walsh?" A man asked.

"May I ask who's calling?" She replied. Her nerves automatically spiked whenever someone responded that way because it usually meant it was something very important and stressful.

"Yes, this is Detective Connors with the Fairview Police Department. Do you have a few minutes to come in and answer a few questions regarding Jack Hastings? His co-workers told me that you're his girlfriend and gave me your number."

Shit!

"Sure, no problem! I can be there in an hour and a half or so. I'm currently in Bakersfield- my grandma needed a ride to the airport. I can be there as soon as I possibly can," she explained.

"No worries. I'll see you in a bit," he confirmed. "Bye."

"Bye," she replied and hung up. She drove out of the airport parking lot so fast that she risked the chance of getting pulled over. She had to speed the entire way back home so she could feed before heading into the police station.

Kyra was able to make it home in fifty minutes, so she had about ten minutes before she had to leave again. She consumed just enough blood to calm her down so she could make it to the police station. Once there, she went to the front desk.

"Hi, I'm Kyra Walsh. I'm here to speak with Detective Connors," she told the officer at the desk.

"Hold on a sec," the officer told her as he went to get the detective. She stood there quietly, wringing her hands so nobody would see how badly they were shaking.

"Hello, Ms. Walsh. Follow me," the tall, muscular detective said, leading her into an interrogation room. He had a murky coloring around him- almost like a shadow that was following close behind.

CHAPTER TWENTY-TWO

"Ms. Walsh, can you describe your relationship with Jack Hastings?" Detective Connors asked.

"He was my boyfriend, but we kept it a secret because he was the paramedic that showed up to my 'incident' at work and he didn't want to get in trouble with his superiors," Kyra replied. She was worried that she had just shared too much, too fast and cringed inwardly.

"I don't see how they could have an issue with that."

"He thought they would see it as unprofessional, and we could have gotten in trouble legally," she said.

"How do you figure?" He asked.

"When I had my incident at work, I had collapsed and hit my head on the pavement. I ended up with short-term memory loss. I couldn't remember anything from that day after I had walked into work. My supervisor was given a misdemeanor, but, if I got my memories back, then I could take her to court for pain and suffering and possibly for assault as well," Kyra explained.

"Wait, what does any of that have to do with Mr. Hastings?"

"He was there for the end of the altercation and he was put down as a witness. He was going to testify if I got my memories back. With us dating openly, that would've made him an unreliable witness because he wouldn't have been able to remain unbiased," she replied.

"Oh, I see... Can I ask you something? If you and Mr. Hastings were romantically involved, then why didn't you report him as a missing person?" He questioned.

"I didn't know he *was* missing. We broke up on the 29th of last month. We had gone to town earlier that day to pack up my things at my parent's house, and then we went grocery shopping so we could make something special for dinner since I was having a bad day," she told him.

"What happened to make you have a bad day? Did you and Mr. Hastings get into an argument?" He asked.

"No. I had been fighting with my mum and Jack was kind enough to let me move in with him until I found another job. You can even ask my mum. Here, I still have several voicemails from her, and I left a note for her at the house telling her where I was and who I was with so she wouldn't worry," she told him as she grabbed her phone from her purse.

"Why would you leave your mother a note if you were fighting? You're an adult, you can leave whenever you wanted to," he asked skeptically.

"Have you met an Irish mom before?" She asked.

"No."

"Irish moms aren't exactly the nicest people when you piss them off. I wanted to make sure that she wouldn't throw my things out of the house. But, also, because I have two younger siblings that I've basically had to raise on my own. Our parents were gone so much for work that I was the one who had to make sure that the kids were bathed, fed, and got to school on time and that they did their homework. I also had to do all of the laundry and housework, plus get myself to school and do my own homework. Then, after I graduated, I got a job with flexible hours so I could still take care of the kids," she explained.

She sure wasn't playing it cool right now. Could she possibly have anything she hadn't told him yet? At this rate, he's going to find her guilty and lock her up forever.

"Okay, let's backtrack a little bit- I don't see what any of this has to do with him. Why did you and Mr. Hastings break up?" He asked.

"That night during dinner, he brought up kids and wanting to start a family. I told him that I was nowhere near ready for that kind of commitment, seeing as how I've practically been a parent when I shouldn't have had to be. I wanted more time to be free and experience life outside of Cork- outside of Oregon. He wasn't happy when I told him about my plans to move back to Ireland for a while and live with my grandmother. Jack got mad at me and told me to leave, so I did. I never told him he couldn't go with me, he just assumed I didn't want him there," she replied.

"So, if he kicked you out, where did you go afterwards?"

"The only place I could go. I went back home with my tail between my legs. I didn't immediately go home because it was too late and I didn't want to wake everyone up, so I got a hotel room and then went home first thing in the morning," she explained.

"I noticed that the car you drove here in was one registered to Mr. Hastings. Care to elaborate?" He questioned.

"My car was a piece of junk that took its last breath while trying to make it up Jack's steep ass driveway. He told me that I could borrow his until I found a job. Of course, it wasn't for free though, I told him that I'd pay for any oil changes, plus gas and any wear and tear," she told him.

"Why would he let you borrow his car after you had just broken up? That doesn't make any sense."

"It wasn't after we broke up, it was when we first started dating. It was the first time I went to his house when my car kicked the bucket," she clarified.

"So why do you still have his car if you had broken up? That's the part I'm not understanding."

"Well how else was I supposed to get back home? It's nearly a thirty- minute drive from his house to mine. Was I just supposed to walk while carrying all my boxes? I was going to keep it until my mom could follow me to his house and give me a ride back home, but her next day off isn't until tomorrow. It was supposed to be yesterday, but a few of the nurses got the flu and my mom got called in to work," she explained.

"What about your dad? Why couldn't he help you out?" He asked.

"He's in Ireland on a business trip. He's normally only home about one week a month."

"So, you're basically both mom and dad to your younger siblings. What did they all do when you left?" He asked.

"Well, my mum took the day off until my dad could fly back. He worked from home until I moved back in, then he flew right back to Ireland," she told him.

"That must have been hard to swallow your pride and move

back home," he stated.

Kyra could feel the walls beginning to close in on her, so she quickly tried changing the subject.

"I don't see how any of this has to do with Jack. May I please go? I don't know how I can be of more help and I have to be at work in less than an hour." Kyra was ready to leave. If she answered any more questions, then she risked him finding out the truth.

"Of course. Thank you for your time, Ms. Walsh. I'll walk you out."

CHAPTER TWENTY-THREE

Kyra let out a sigh of relief. She thought for sure that she had slipped up towards the end there.

"Ms. Walsh? One last question. How old are you?" The detective asked. Kyra froze.

"I'm twenty-one, almost twenty-two. Why?" She asked.

"No, you're *new* age."

He had barely whispered *that* word, but Kyra heard it as if he had shouted it from across an empty room.

"What are you talking about?" She asked, trying to play dumb because there was no way this man could possibly know (or even believe) that people like her really exist.

He looked around to make sure no one was watching and then used his fingers to mimic fangs. Kyra's blood went ice cold.

Oh shit!...

"Don't worry, I knew about Jack. He needed someone on his

161

side for when he got out of control. So, what really happened to him? Did he attack you?" He asked. It took her a moment, but she eventually nodded, afraid to speak.

"You killed him, didn't you?" He whispered.

"I didn't have a choice… He was going to kill me if I didn't kill him first. I saw it." Kyra's voice cracked and she started to cry.

"Come on, let me walk you out," the detective said quietly as he ushered Kyra to the door. He walked her to her car and opened her door for her.

"Look, I know you did what you had to do to survive, but you need to be more careful. I could tell what you were the second you walked into the station. You'll be lucky if I'm the only outsider who knows what you are. To save both of our asses, I'll take care of the Jack situation. You'll need to stay away from his house for a few days while I clear everything up. After that, you'll be free to go over there whenever you'd like," he explained.

"What are you going to do?" She asked.

"It's best if you don't know any details. Why don't you go home and follow your routine as closely as possible. Don't clear your location on any of your devices, including the GPS in the car- that will only look more suspicious. Most importantly, try not to let yourself over think any of this because people who over think tend to make mistakes."

"Detective?"

"Yes, Ms. Walsh?"

"Something really bad is coming. Something big. I don't know when, but it'll be soon…"

"Excuse me? It that a threat?!" He questioned.

"No, sir! Not at all! Did Jack talk to you about me after I was turned?" She asked.

"Not a word. Why?"

"I wasn't human before I was turned, I was a witch. I come from a long line of Pagan witches who have a strong pull towards the earth and nature. Whatever is coming, it's going to be apocalyptic. A lot of people are going to be scared and lash out. I suggest having six months' worth of canned food and other staples at home to be on the safe side. I'm also planning on turning Jack's place into a type of bunker, somewhere where a select amount of people can take shelter. You and your family will be more than welcome to stay there. Until then, I suggest slowly stocking up each week and put as much money into savings as possible," she explained.

"Are you sure something's coming?" He asked skeptically.

"I'm positive. I'll try and keep you updated if I find out anything else. I'm still trying to develop my abilities, so there's no guarantee I'll be able to find out more."

"I'll take your word for it, Ms. Walsh. Expect a phone call from me within the next few days. Now, go home and try to relax," he told her.

"Thank you, detective."

He nodded and shut her car door for her before walking back into the station. He turned back to look at her before going back into the police station.

Kyra sat there for several minutes while she tried to relax. She felt like she had just been on an emotional roller-coaster and it freaked her out. Her emotions were all over the place compared to when she was 'human.' She had less than an hour until she had to be to work so there wasn't enough time for her to go back home and change clothes. She had been so distracted by having to go to the police station, that she had completely forgotten to put a spare set of clothes in the car. Kyra then drove down the road to *Ross* and kept her fingers crossed that they had what she needed.

Once inside the store, she kept her head down to avoid direct eye contact with anyone. She made her way over to the dress pant section and almost immediately found three pairs in her size, so she walked over to the shirts. They didn't have a great selection of blouses, but she was able to find a couple that would be passable to wear to work. She was lucky enough to have her work shoes on, so she didn't have to worry about that part.

Thankfully, she no longer felt the need to wear makeup because that would've gotten expensive very fast. Even though she had money in savings she could use to buy herself more work clothes, she was on a budget and didn't want to be flat broke before payday since she had forgotten to ask when that would be. Kyra was mentally kicking herself for forgetting to ask that important question.

Kyra wasn't too worried about finding her own place anymore since she could live at Jack's house once things were taken care of. If her mom got upset about her moving out because she'd need someone to watch the kids, then oh well. They weren't Kyra's kids; they were her siblings. She shouldn't have to be responsible for them because she wasn't their parent. Kyra was done playing the mommy role to her own siblings. She was ready to be her own person.

She was in such a foul mood when she finally got up to one of the registers that she had to use her customer service voice so she wouldn't freak out the cashier. She hurriedly paid for her things and rushed out to her car. One thing she had completely forgotten to consider was that she now needed to find somewhere she could change her clothes...

There was only one option since she was cutting it really close to being late. She'd have to change in the car... She was internally grateful for the fact that Jack's car had tinted windows because she should be able to go unseen as long as she stayed crouched down in the backseat. First, she'd have to find somewhere slightly more secluded than the mall parking lot, just to air on the side of caution.

There was a vacant building a few blocks over that had its own parking lot, so she pulled in and parked before climbing over the seats to the backseat. She took the tags off the clothes she was going to wear- not caring that her outfit wasn't going to match. The only part that matters is that she doesn't break the dress code on only her second day.

She quickly changed her clothes, then climbed back into the driver's seat. Kyra was going to be cutting it really close today and her anxiety was doing a great job of reminding her of that every two seconds. She was hoping she'd have enough time to get something to eat beforehand, but, as it was, she'd be arriving at work with maybe five minutes before she had to clock in. Even though she was only working a five-hour shift, she was worried about her hunger getting out of control.

Kyra was supposed to feed again before work because she wasn't able to go more than six hours in between each feeding. Well, more like she hadn't gone that long since she was turned. She hoped that maybe she could get some snacks from the nearby mini-mart on her break and that it would tide her over until she could get home.

She made it to work with seven minutes to spare, so she allowed herself a couple of minutes to sit in the car and collect her composure. She needed to calm her thoughts so she could focus on her job and hopefully make it through the shift without harming anyone. Kyra reminded herself that she was the strongest person in existence and could do anything she put her mind to.

CHAPTER TWENTY-FOUR

Kyra luckily made it to the end of her shift without killing anyone, but she'd had a tough time focusing on what Fiona was trying to teach her. She hoped nobody noticed her change in behavior, but couldn't be sure since no one brought it up. She was still able to retain new information, but her reaction time felt way slower to her.

The moment after clocking out, Kyra rushed out to her car and sped the whole way home. She desperately needed to feed before she attacked an innocent human. People honked at her the whole way home as she sped through traffic, but she ignored them. The normal twenty-five-minute drive somehow ended up being only eighteen minutes. Kyra was so thirst crazed that she didn't care who got in her way.

Once in her room, Kyra threw her closet door open, tossing everything to the side, and ripped the fridge open. Before she could stop herself, she had poked a hole in the first blood bag, completely draining it. The taste of the blood sent her into a downward spiral, making her more bloodthirsty.

She was halfway through the second bag when the phone in her pocket buzzed, snapping her out of the blood lust. Kyra grabbed her phone and saw that Thomas had texted her wondering where she was. She looked down at herself to see a small trail of blood on her new blouse from where it had dripped down her chin. Kyra texted him back, telling him that she had gone home to change clothes and that she would be over in a few minutes.

Kyra scurried around her room, hurrying to get rid of the evidence from her sudden loss of self-control. She didn't want her mom to find the bloody shirt, so she wadded it up and threw it under her bed. Kyra put on a t-shirt, sweatpants, and a hoodie, before running back out the door.

She wanted to run over, but she couldn't take the risk of being seen, so she got in the car and drove the quarter-mile to Thomas's house. He was waiting outside for her when she pulled up and her heart skipped a beat.

Even though he was dressed the same as he always was, she kept noticing new things about his appearance that she had never noticed before. Like the fact that his eyes were a light shade of brown, kind of like warm honey- or that his lips were full and smooth, like they had never been chapped a single day in his whole life. Overall, he just just seemed very well manicured- like he took very good care of himself and put a lot of work into maintaining his appearance and physical well-being.

He caught Kyra checking him out from her safe space inside the car and he grinned, revealing his perfectly straight, white teeth. The perfect teeth that he'd had his whole life because he was one of those rare people who were lucky enough to have never had to have braces when they were growing up.

Kyra took a deep breath before slowly getting out of the car. She met him on the front porch and he picked her up, swinging her in a circle as he kissed her. As their kiss became more heated, Thomas froze and pulled away.

"Hey, what's wrong?" She asked.

"Did you feed on someone before coming over?" He asked her with a tone of disgust.

"No, but I did feed from a blood bag... Why?" She was suddenly as nervous as she was last night when she was last over here. He set her back down on her own feet and her legs nearly gave out under her.

"Are you telling me the truth?" He questioned. She could tell he was skeptical so she decided to tell him everything.

"Yes, I am. I didn't have time to feed before work so I ended up going a little overboard... Here, let me show you," she told him. He nodded and stood still.

"Not here. Let's go inside," she said as she ushered him through the front door. She didn't want to take any chances one of his neighbors might witness their strange interaction. Once inside, he stood still again and didn't say a word. It was a lot easier this time now that she knew what she was doing. She started with early that morning when she went to Jack's house, then when she took her grandma to the airport.

Kyra spent close to ten minutes showing him her memories. She had focused a lot more on the memories from when she was at the police station so Thomas could know exactly what was going on with the Jack situation. They opened their eyes and Kyra could see that Thomas was clearly upset, but about which part?

"What's coming?" He asked suddenly, throwing Kyra off guard.

"Excuse me? I need a little more than that to go on," she replied.

"When you were talking to the detective, you said that something bad was coming- but what is it?" He asked.

"I'm not sure... All I know is that it has to do with nature somehow. My grandma told me that humans have thrown nature out of balance and it's about to take back control. What I do know is that soon it won't be very safe to go outside," Kyra explained.

"But, for how long?" He asked in a sad voice. Thomas hated being cooped up inside for long periods of time. He was one of the most active, outdoorsy people she had ever met, which is probably what attracted her to him- her being a witch of the earth and all that fun stuff.

"I'm not sure," she replied honestly. "But at least we'll have each other," she said as she hugged him. He hugged her back and Kyra could hear his heart racing. He picked her up again, but this time he carried her to his room. He set her on the bed and removed her shoes, then walked over and turned on the tv. He always somehow seemed to know exactly what she needed to make her happy or feel better when she was feeling down.

"What would you like to watch? You can pick this time, as long as it's not some lame documentary again!" He teased as he handed her the remote.

"Hey, baby animals are adorable, okay!" She laughed as she aimed a pillow at his head. He dodged it, laughing as he left the room. Kyra could hear him making popcorn in the kitchen but she did her best to ignore him as she sneakily turned on *The Vampire Diaries*.

She had finally convinced him to watch it a while back and she knew he secretly liked it even though he complained every time she as much as mentioned a line or scene from the show. Now it seemed as if those complains were becoming fewer and further in between.

"Seriously, this again? Never mind, I'll take that documentary again- you know, the one with the fish," Thomas laughed as he came back in the room carrying two big bowls.

"What?" She laughed at him. "I thought we could do some research on me," she joked. "So, what did you bring me?"

"I brought *us* a bowl of popcorn to share, but I also brought you a bowl of ice cream- your favorite," he told her as he leaned down to kiss her.

"Why thank you, kind sir," she giggled as she kissed him again.

Their intimate affections were still so knew to each other that Kyra got butterflies in her stomach every time Thomas so much as glanced at her. One would think that their years of friendship would make things a lot easier, but that was furthest from the truth.

"You are very welcome, my lady," he replied as he handed her the ice cream. Of course, he knew her favorite kind and always had some stocked in his freezer all year long because he knew she was crazy about it. Just one of the many things she had always loved about him.

They had started watching *The Vampire Diaries* right after the incident with Meghan because Thomas wanted to help keep her mind off of it. She knew he would have still given in eventually to watch it with her because he usually ended up just giving her whatever she wanted. He wasn't a total pushover, he just genuinely enjoyed making her happy. Now she knew why.

Kyra leaned her head against Thomas's shoulder as they watched their show. He held her hand under the covers, stroking the back of her hand with his thumb. It felt so nice being with him that Kyra's worries slowly began to fade as she relaxed into him, laying her head on his chest. He kissed the top of her head and wrapped his arms around her, creating a protective shield around her and making her feel safe.

CHAPTER TWENTY-FIVE

Kyra awoke several hours later to being Thomas's little spoon. Her eyes flashed open wide in shock when she realized what had just happened.

She had just slept for the first time in eight days and she didn't even know what to think about it. Was it a bad thing? Was it a sign that she's starting to die again? Did she somehow develop a new ability? Regardless, it felt nice to sleep, especially next to the man she loves more than anything in the world.

She was surprised to find herself feeling fully rested with zero grogginess whatsoever. In the past, whenever she had pulled an all-nighter and finally got caught up on sleep, she would feel so exhausted as if she had once again stayed awake yet another night.

Thomas hadn't woken up yet, so Kyra took the opportunity to lay there and bask in the joy of peaceful sleep and new love. Nothing else mattered in that moment, and Kyra felt like everything in the world was okay again. She was full of bliss- nothing less.

Over the next three days, Kyra went back and forth between work and Thomas's house. She had been able to sleep every one of those nights and they were both amazed. She had no idea what had started it, but she didn't care because now all she ever wanted to do was sleep in case it was only temporary.

When Kyra got off work that Saturday evening, she saw that she had a text from an unsaved number. Normally, she would delete random texts without reading them, but something told her not to do it this time. She opened it to see that it was from Detective Connors. It said that it was now safe to go back to Jack's house and to not ask any questions. He also told her that there was an envelope on Jack's desk for her, but he didn't know what was inside.

She felt odd having any sort of connection to a corrupt cop, but there was nothing she could do about it right now, unfortunately. Plus, it wasn't her place to judge him because who knows what happened in his life to require him to work for a wealthy serial killer. Who knows, maybe it wasn't his choice at all- maybe Jack manipulated his mind and now that he's dead, Detective Connors is probably trying to right the wrongs that were committed against him.

Kyra texted Thomas to let him know she'd be there later, then she headed to Jack's house. The drive felt longer this time because she was nervous about going back to that place. She had felt a very strange energy in the house the last time she was there and it had freaked her out to the point that she had to leave. It had felt like someone was watching her, but she knew there was no one in the house. She'd call her grandma tomorrow and ask how to do a cleansing ritual on the house.

As Kyra was pulling up to the house, she could feel the hair on the back of her neck stand up. Maybe she should've had Thomas come with her... She took a deep breath before stepping over the threshold, entering the house for possibly the last time. That feeling didn't go away- in fact it got worse the closer she got to her room. Maybe it was just her anxiety, or maybe some lingering guilt over killing Jack. Either way, she was *not* going back in that room! She didn't care that she still had things inside. She'd rather buy all new stuff than ever have to open that door.

Kyra walked as calmly as she could manage towards his office, not stopping until she got to his desk. She sat down in the desk chair and opened the flat, manila envelope that had her name printed across the front. The feeling of unease still hadn't subsided as she dumped out the contents of the envelope. Her jaw dropped as she read everything.

Inside was the deed to the house and land put in her name, plus the titles to all of the vehicles. Along with that, she had been named beneficiary to his bank accounts which totaled up to $80,000! She couldn't believe what she was seeing. Why would Jack leave everything to her when they had never officially dated? How could he have known to do any of this? Every document in the envelope had been dated as the same day she was kidnapped, including the suicide note that was signed by Jack himself.

Kyra was mentally retracing her steps, thinking back to that day, but the only way he could have gotten all that stuff done is if he had done it all before he ran her off the road. According to Jack, he had never left her side after the 'accident' because he was worried that things might've gone south while he was away. Kyra didn't doubt him because of how obsessive he was of her. That only left the question: Who had the envelope this whole time?

"Kyra..."

Her head whipped around at the sound of her name, but no one was there. She couldn't even hear the sound of someone breathing. It had been as quiet as a whisper, but she *knew* she heard someone calling her name. She was *definitely* being watched- that she knew for sure.

"Over here..." Kyra nearly leapt out of her skin. The voice was coming from the mirror on the wall next to her. She slowly got up from the chair and crept over to the mirror to inspect it. It was all cloudy like an antique mirror, but instead of seeing her own reflection, there was a slight outline of a man in what looked to be a forest.

"H-Hello?" She stuttered. "What are you?" She asked fearfully. Every instinct in her body was telling her to run, but for some reason she was frozen in place.

"What? You mean, you don't recognize me?" He asked as Jack's face suddenly appeared. Kyra screamed and fell backwards in horror. She was *terrified*.

This can't be real! This is just some prank or something, she thought to herself.

"B-but how?" She asked, too terrified to get out more than two words.

"Well, as you can see, I'm dead. But what you probably didn't know is that when one supernatural being kills another, they get stuck in purgatory. So, here I am until who knows when. Thanks for that, by the way," he sneered. Kyra got back on her feet and looked him directly in the eye.

"Why did you lie to me?" She asked. She didn't dare move

this time.

"You gotta be a bit more specific, love," he replied.

"Why did you lie about being a good person? Why did you lie when I asked if you had ever killed anyone?" She questioned.

"I never lied to you, Kyra. I didn't necessarily tell you the truth, but I never flat out lied to you- I just withheld the truth," he smirked.

"Semantics! That's still lying. I only have one more question before I leave. Why did you put everything you own in my name? I know you never thought I could ever kill you, so why?" She asked. He stared at her like the answer should be obvious. He sighed.

"I did it because I was telling you the truth when I told you that I love you. I knew that Detective Connors was finding it harder to cover up my mistakes, so I prepared like I was going to be hunted down and killed. It's a good thing I did, or you'd be totally screwed right now."

"What's that supposed to mean?" She asked.

"If I hadn't already had a plan in place, then you would currently be sitting in jail right now for my murder," he explained.

"Lucky me..." She rolled her eyes, then walked back over to the desk and put everything back in the envelope.

"Wait! Where are you going?" He asked.

"Home, Jack. I'm done listening to your bullshit. Have a nice afterlife," she said as she turned around.

"So, you don't want to hear about the new plague?" Kyra turned around and glared at him.

"What are you talking about?" She questioned. She was completely fed up with his lies and manipulation. He smirked and Kyra suddenly got the feeling that he wasn't lying anymore.

At least not this time…

CHAPTER TWENTY-SIX

"What are you talking about?" Kyra asked. She really didn't want to hear him out, but she couldn't take the chance that he knew something she didn't. She was trying her best to protect her mind from whatever head game is was trying to play on her, but something in his voice was telling her that what he said was the truth.

"A plague is coming for all of humanity. Do you remember learning about the Spanish Influenza outbreak of 1918 in history class?" Jack asked.

"Yeah, what about it?" She asked through a clenched jaw.

"It'll be like that, but that won't be all."

"Could you be any more cryptic?" She huffed.

"It will be the beginning of the end. I'm sorry, but I can't give you any specifics or it could change the future in the wrong direction," he explained.

"Like the butterfly effect?" She asked.

"Exactly. I honestly wish I could tell you more, but I've already said too much," he told her.

"Well, thanks for the help...not." Kyra rolled her eyes. Why would he even bother contacting her if he wasn't going to tell her anything useful?

"Look, I've seen what happens if I tell you everything. The world will come to an end- as in every living thing will be gone, completely wiped off the face of the earth."

"How can you possibly know that when it hasn't happened yet?" She asked.

"Because she showed me," he replied.

"Who did?" She asked.

"Freya."

"As in the Celtic goddess?!" She asked, eyes wide in disbelief. He nodded.

"I don't believe you," she spat out.

"Believe what you want, but I'm telling you the truth."

"Goodbye, Jack," Kyra said as she left the office.

"Please don't leave..." He pleaded. Kyra stopped in the doorway before turning back to look at him.

"Move on, Jackson. Don't stay in purgatory just to keep an eye on me because I'm not coming back... Goodbye, Jack." Kyra left the office and never looked back. She was done with that part of her life and she was finally ready to start anew. She would face whatever was to come and with the people she loves most by her side.

Twenty-Seven

Mr. Walsh

The sins of the father...

I love Kyra more than anything in the world, but I can't help but feel like I've failed her. I should have told her the truth of her parentage a long time ago. There isn't anything I wouldn't do to be able to go back in time and never date Sheila again. Dating your own sibling (whether or not you know you're siblings) is disgusting and there's a reason why it goes against the laws of nature. It's a miracle that Kyra turned out normal. Unfortunately, for her, she never got the chance to meet her twin sister. Sheila told me that Nora had been born way smaller than Kyra was so sickly that she only lived for mere minutes after birth.

On a positive note, Kyra was the best child anyone could ever ask for. She was such a quiet and easy baby that started sleeping through the night at only two months old. Then, as she got older, she hardly ever made noises and she kept herself entertained. Sometimes I wondered if she was even human because I had never heard of any other babies being so mellow.

I'm just hoping that once Kyra has gotten the chance to spend a good amount of time away from her mother, she can blossom into the young woman I know she can be. At that point, hopefully she'll be ready to know the whole truth- the truth about why I really spend so much time in Ireland. Now isn't the time for that though. Kyra has endured so much already and has too much on her plate right now, but maybe soon that will change and I can tell her all about my life.

Twenty-Eight

Mrs. Walsh

Why did it have to be me and not her? Why did the magic have to skip a generation? Why couldn't I have had powers? What is so wrong with me that the universe and everyone in it hates me so goddamn much? It's all my mom's fault anyway. She never told me I had a brother, so how was I to know that I had been dating my own half brother? And that's *my* fault?!

I swear, Kyra is the daughter my mother wishes she'd had. They were so close from the second she was born, which is why we moved to the United States in the first place, so I could put some distance between the two of them. She never really felt like my daughter anyway. I barely remember giving birth to her. Kyra has always felt like a parasite- leaching away any magic that I may have possibly had. Thankfully, we don't look that much alike like some mothers and daughters do.

Sometimes I feel horrible for feeling these things about my own daughter, but then I remind myself about the fact that I am human and she is not. Anyone who practices witchcraft is evil and needs to seek medical attention because they are sick in the head. Believing in some random god/goddess isn't healthy. They don't exist- if they did, then the world probably wouldn't be such a shitty place because there would be a lot of "other beings" to keep humans in order.

The day Kyra came back after 'moving in' with some random guy, I could tell that something was wrong. She no longer looked like my daughter, she looked ethereal- like someone who had been touched with an enormous amount of power. Ever since that day, there has actually been a thin veil of peace in our house. It's hard to explain, but, ever since that day, the fogginess in my mind has lifted and I've finally started to feel more like my old self. The version of me I was back before Kyra was born.

Maybe now we might start to work on our mother-daughter relationship. If I'm being honest, I've hated the person I've been these past twenty years or so. I felt like the real version of me was locked up deep in my mind and that horrible version was a stranger that had taken over my mind and body. For the first time in my entire adult life, I finally feel free... almost...

Twenty-Nine

Detective Connors

For the first time in a long while, I finally felt like my mind was my own again. It wasn't until I received the call about Jack's death that I realized what had been wrong with me. My best guess was that he had used his freaky, weirdo vampire powers on me and had been using me like puppet. It felt like a violation and if he weren't already dead, I would kill him myself.

All I wanted now was to take a hot shower- the hotter the better- and get whatever he did to me, out of my mind. If it were safe to bathe in bleach, I'd probably do that too.

When Jack died and I found out about Kyra, I was scared to make the phone call to have her come down to the police station. He had never mentioned her before- or at least not that I could remember- so I had no idea if she was anything like him. For all I knew, she could've picked up where Jack left off and turn me back into a puppet.

The moment she walked into the police station, my initial

reaction was fear; the kind of fear that nearly froze me in place. But, once we were alone in the interrogation room, that feeling suddenly changed to a warm feeling- as if I had been standing next to a fire. She almost looked like she was glowing even though she had a gaunt look to her eyes. I can only imagine what Jack had put her through.

Honestly, I felt a little bad for her after our short conversation. It was obvious to me that she had been dealt an unfair hand in life, so I felt bad for having to interrogate her even though it's literally my job to investigate those closest to someone who's been murdered. She reminded me so much of my two daughters that it was hard to stay focused because I wanted to tuck her under my arm and keep her safe.

After the interrogation, I noticed how everyone in the room seemed to be fixated on Kyra and it made me very nervous. I made a point to escort her to her car to hopefully prevent anyone from approaching her. If they were to show any real interest in her, it was likely they could find out that I became corrupt and I could be thrown in jail with all the people I've worked very hard to arrest over the years.

So, when she was getting into her car and she then informed me about something bad coming, I didn't dare doubt her because who knows what kind of powers vampires can have. I have never been the curious type, and I wasn't planning on changing that any time soon. Hopefully she's wrong about whatever it is, but I doubt it because of the things I've already seen changing. Even I've already changed more than I thought I would've. With the most recent election, I voted Democrat for the first time in my entire adult life. It was either that, or not vote at all and I wasn't about to let them take control over me like that. In my opinion, *Trump* is nothing more than a glorified celebrity/ *Oompa Loompa* wannabe.

I know that makes me seem like a "traitor" or a fake Republican, but he was never even a politician to begin with and has absolutely no place being in politics. There was also no way I was going to vote for a clown that was going to take away the rights of my daughters just because they're women. My daughters are so smart and both have more common sense than most of the men I work with.

Kyra would actually make a wonderful role model for both of my daughters in my opinion. She kinda gave off the vibe of being able to create big changes in the world. I'm looking forward to see what comes of her. She is destined for big things.

Thirty

Jack Hastings

She'll be back... she has to come back. If I mess things up with Kyra and do something to knock her off her path, Freya made it very clear what would become of me- and I really don't feel like wandering alone in nothingness for the rest of eternity.

I wish I had kept my cool and gotten her to believe what I told her because, if she doesn't come back, the rest of humanity will be doomed. And when I say doomed, I mean that there will absolutely be no way to save what will be left of humanity five years from now.

I honestly could have lived out the rest of eternity without ever having to see what happens next. It was like watching those videos in history class of reenactments of all the wars- and yes, including all the bloody, gory details...

I can't speak for everyone when I say that humanity has become a disease, but the truth is in the facts. There's something so catastrophic that will happen four years from now that the rich and powerful will try and sweep it under the rug. Innocent men, women, and children will be wiped off the face of the earth- just because some rich, white people want the land that they're living on. But, because of the day and age that we live in, people around the world will be able to see all the blood and death as if they themselves were there, but without having to leave the comfort of their own homes.

This is why Kyra needs to continue on her path. My purpose is to keep her focused and on track so that she can help prevent disasters like that from ever coming to fruition. From what I've seen of the near future, I am honestly kinda glad that Kyra killed me… I mean, it does suck being dead and being stuck somewhere in the middle and not being able to pass on, but it sure as hell beats what's to come.

I'm hoping Kyra is strong enough to affect enough change in the world that the future I've seen gets completely changed. I know she's strong enough physically, but mentally and emotionally- I'm not so sure… Kyra was always a very empathetic person from what I saw, so I have no clue how she's going to react to the events to come.

Only time will tell, I guess…

Notes

CHAPTER FOUR

1   Mother? Where am I? Why are you crying?

2   He can't lie to her about the results from her MRI because she could sue him for malpractice- so he doesn't tell her anything and keeps it to himself.

CHAPTER FIVE

3   Pun + Funny = Punny

Should she stay, or should she go?

Her soulmate- or the existence of humankind?

Decisions, decisions. What will she choose?

Find out in the next installment of The Cork Chronicles- coming soon in 2026.

Think you know how book two will end? Then you would be very wrong. Life is no fairytale- not even in a perfect world. Just like life, this story is full of ups and downs and surprises that you would least expect.

I want every reader to feel like they have a connection to at least one character or the story as a whole. My wish is to represent every single type of person in my stories because we're all in this world together, which makes us more alike than everyone would think. This world would be a much better place if everyone opened their minds and their hearts to their fellow person. Hopefully, my stories will help enlighten people to at least *try* to broaden their minds and care a little more for those around them.

Remember everyone, we are in this together- for better or worse. So why not fight like hell to make it better? I love y'all!

About the Author

A single mom still trying to find her place in the world. I have been obsessed with books and writing since I was six years old and it has been my lifelong dream to become a successful writer.

I am AuDHD and I would never change that about myself as it allows me to see the world in a much different way. It's like living in a magical land where everything I imagine can come to life.

My goal with this series is to help create a sense of community again and to provide an escape to those who need it. I also want to prove to myself that I am always worth it and to show my child that they can accomplish anything they set their mind to.

I even created a Spotify playlist specifically for this series that I am constantly adding to: The Cork Chronicles Soundtrack

You can connect with me on:

🐦 https://twitter.com/PaigeHartwick

🔗 https://www.tiktok.com/@trickyhartwicky2.0